Suspended

Suspended

Robert Rayner

James Lorimer & Company Ltd., Publishers
Toronto

James Lorimer & Company Ltd. acknowledges the support of the Ontario Arts Council. We acknowledge the support of the Government of Canada through the Book Publishing Industry Development Program (BPIDP) for our publishing activities. We acknowledge the support of the Canada Council for the Arts for our publishing program. We acknowledge the support of the Government of Ontario through the Ontario Media Development Corporation's Ontario Book Initiative.

Cover illustration:Greg Ruhl

Library and Archives Canada Cataloguing in Publication
Rayner, Robert, 1946-
    Suspended / written by Robert Rayner

(Sports stories; 75))
ISBN-13: 978-1-55028-861-2 (boards)
ISBN-10: 1-55028-861-X (boards)
ISBN-13: 978-1-55028-860-5 (pbk.)
ISBN-10: 1-55028-860-1 (pbk.)

I. Title. II. Series: Sports stories (Toronto, Ont.); 75.

| PS8585.A974S86 2004 | jC813.'6 | C2004-904824-4 |

James Lorimer & Company Ltd.,	Distributed in the United States by
Publishers	Orca Book Publishers
317 Adelaide St. West	P.O. Box 468
Suite 1002	Custer, WA USA
Toronto, Ontario	98240-0468
M5V 1P9	
www.lorimer.ca	

Printed and bound in Canada.

CONTENTS

For Owen

Thanks to Gerald Smerdon,
Educational Psychologist,
for advice on character types.

1 Brawl

The last thing Grandad said as I left to play soccer was, "Don't let them drag you down to their level. Remember the rules of the game."

So when Hawler the Mauler crushed Flyin' Brian's hand, and I started the brawl, I knew I'd have to keep it a secret from Grandad.

Brunswick Valley School's games against St. Croix Middle School are always tough, but this one had been ferocious. Brian, our goalkeeper, had been pushed several times before the Mauler stepped on his hand. Tiny Jones had tripped Julie and pulled her long, blond hair when she tackled him. The St. Croix players and spectators had teased us throughout the game. Whenever our fullback Toby — who's a bit overweight — got the ball, they'd yell, "Yay, Fats!" and "Go, Lard boy!" They taunted Julie by chanting "Blondie" every time she touched the ball.

I hate getting dragged into a fight, because there's

never any glory in it, only bruises and bad feelings. And I hate going against the rules of the game. Rules are rules, as Grandad always says. But as captain of a soccer team I can't stand by and watch the other side trample on my goalie. So when the Mauler stamped on Brian's fingers, then grinned at his team mates, I head-butted him in the stomach. I didn't even think about it — which was probably good, because I might have changed my mind, seeing as Hawler's bigger than me. While he was doubled up, I grabbed his hair and was about to mash his face with my knee when his sidekick, Doozie Dougan, grabbed me from behind.

Hawler snarled, "You asked for this, Shay Sutton."

The referee blew his whistle, but it was too late.

I saw Hawler aim his fist toward my stomach, but Magic, one of our forwards, appeared and took the blow in his open hand without flinching. At the same time Dougan gasped, released me, and collapsed.

"Are you okay, Shay?" Toby asked. He leaned over Dougan and said, "Sorry, Doozie. I didn't mean to hit you so hard."

Doozie growled and lunged at Toby, while Hawler swung at Magic. The referee's whistle sounded louder this time. Toby tumbled backwards, grabbing Doozie and taking him down with him, while Magic, weaving smoothly, easily avoided Hawler.

The referee ordered, "Time out, Brunswick Valley! Go to your bench. You, too, St. Croix. Coaches, get your teams under control."

Miss Little, our coach, pushed her big round glasses back — they were always slipping down her nose — and shook her finger at us, scolding, "Now, children. You know that is not the way to behave."

That's how she talks to us — as if we were little kids. She talked to us like that in kindergarten and she still talks to us that way. It's as if we're still five years old. If we didn't like Miss Little so much for other things it'd probably drive us crazy. But as it is, we don't mind. In fact, we kind of like it.

Miss Little flapped her hands, shooing us towards our bench as if we were a herd of sheep.

As all the players headed off, the referee threatened, "I'll be reporting this disgraceful exhibition to both your principals."

The St. Croix coach lectured his players, "I've warned you before about fighting ..."

Hawler interrupted. "They started it. Shay Sutton butted me for no reason."

The St. Croix coach called, "You heard that, referee. They started it."

The referee turned to Miss Little. "Your players started the brawl."

Miss Little retorted, "They were provoked."

"I don't care if they were provoked. They started

the brawl, and I hold Brunswick Valley School responsible for it," the referee said.

Hauler and Doozie smirked.

The referee decided to end the game, since there
were only two minutes left and the score was level.

We sat on our bench, heads hanging. Everyone
knew we'd let down Miss Little. She's always taught us
to play with dignity and grace, no matter what happens in the game. I sneaked a look at her. She was
standing in front of us with her hands clasped.

I guessed it was my job as captain to say something.
"Sorry, Miss Little."

Toby, beside me, mumbled, "Sorry, Miss L." Julie,
on the other side, said, "We forgot about dignity and
grace, didn't we?"

A chorus of apologies followed from the rest of the
team.

Miss Little sighed. "That's all right, dears. You were
seriously provoked. Let's just hope the principal sees it
that way."

2 Code of Conduct

But it didn't matter what Mr. Justason, the principal at Brunswick Valley School, thought.

Instead of calling him, the referee called Mrs. Stuart, the chair of the school district council. She called Ms. Dugalici, the district director of schools, who in turn called Mr. Justason. By that time our ten-second scuffle had become World War III.

French was first the next morning, and we were hardly in our seats when Mr. Justason's voice sounded over the intercom. "All members of the soccer team report to my office immediately."

As the six soccer players in our Grade 7 class rose to leave, Ms. Watkins, the French teacher, warned us, "Mr. Justason has the director of schools with him and I believe they're both quite upset …"

Ms. Watkins is tall and scrawny. When she walks around the classroom she looks like a heron, with her head and neck lurching ahead of her legs.

Brian was doing a shuffle dance between the desks as he came from the back, snapping his fingers and making a "Boom-chucka-chucka-boom-boom-sssh-sssh" sound. His hair bounced with the rhythm of his drumming.

"... and you might be wise not to make the situation worse," Ms. Watkins finished, looking at Brian.

The rest of the team was spilling into the hallway, so we headed downstairs in a bunch.

Little Linh-Mai, Toby's fullback partner, whose head barely reaches our shoulders, groaned, "Are we in trouble with Mr. Justason?"

"No, he just wants to tell us to have a good day," said Toby.

The twins, Jillian and Jessica, who are in Grade 6 with Linh-Mai, giggled at Toby's comment, their blond ponytails bobbing. Linh-Mai joined in, and with Brian still doing drum sounds, we were quite noisy as we came in sight of the principal's office.

Mr. Justason was standing in the hallway. "Quiet!" he barked, and pointed to an empty classroom across the hallway. "We'll meet in there."

Toby tried, "How-de-doody, Mr. Justason."

"I said be quiet!" the principal thundered.

We filed into the classroom. Ms. Dugalici and Mrs. Stuart stood on opposite sides of the room.

Mrs. Stuart is big and bony, and always wears long, plain dresses. She lives next door to the school, and seems to be in her garden every recess, frowning and shaking her head as she watches the playground. Several times she's complained to Mr. Justason about student behaviour, calling him over when he was on duty. She's accused girls of wearing tops that were too short, boys of wearing T-shirts with inappropriate messages, and both of using bad language, fighting, and making too much noise.

Mr. Justason always says, "I agree with you, Mrs. Stuart. I'll talk to the students about it."

But he never does.

At the back of the room, Miss Little was sitting in a desk with her chin in her hands.

Mr. Justason followed us in and ordered, "Sit!"

"Next, he'll be asking us to fetch and heel," whispered Toby.

"Do you have anything to say, Toby Morton?" asked Mr. Justason.

"No more than usual," said Toby.

Mr. Justason stood at the front of the class, arms folded and glaring. "You are in enough trouble already without making matters worse by being rude."

He's been principal for only about six weeks, since September. He used to be the vice principal at the high school, so it's quite a change for him coming to little Brunswick Valley School, with only two hundred students from kindergarten to Grade 8. I've never seen him smile.

Mr. Justason paced backwards and forwards at the front of the room. That's how he walks around the school — stern and serious. He must get his clothes at the Tall Man clothing store because nowhere else would have anything long enough. His head looks too small for his tall body.

Mr. Justason smoothed his hair, which is shiny, wavy and brushed straight back. Julie says he uses Grecian Formula, to stop him going gray.

"I'm disappointed with your behaviour at the game yesterday," he started. "Mrs. Stuart and Ms. Dugalici are here because they're equally upset. Mrs. Stuart has the referee's report, which she has shared with Ms. Dugalici and me, on your fight with the St. Croix team."

"It was their fault," I protested. "They provoked us."

"I don't need comments or excuses," Mr. Justason replied briskly. "Your conduct reflects badly on the school and on the whole community. I could suspend all of you from playing soccer for the rest of the year."

He looked at Ms. Dugalici.

Beside Mr. Justason and Mrs. Stuart, Ms. Dugalici is a shrimp — a very scary shrimp. She rarely speaks, and when she does, it's not much more than a whisper. Her short, dark hair is so tight, it looks as if it's been sprayed on her head. She dresses like a business person and always wears dark glasses.

Ms. Dugalici nodded.

We'd met her before. When she was put in charge of all the schools, she came to our opening assembly and told us the discipline at Brunswick Valley needed improvement.

Mr. Justason stood waiting for her to speak. It was strange seeing him deal with *his* boss.

In a slow voice more menacing than if she'd shouted at us, the director said, "I came here today to let you know how seriously I regard this affair. I have warned you already that student behaviour has to improve. Now Mr. Justason tells me he has a new discipline plan. I suggest you listen carefully to what he has to say."

She looked at Mr. Justason, and quietly left the room. He continued: "I have decided to give you a second chance — on condition that you promise to obey the new Players' Code of Conduct."

"What's that?" I asked.

"The Players' Code of Conduct is part of what I call our Drive for Discipline," the principal explained. Mrs. Stuart nodded and smiled. "The Code outlines the terms under which students may represent their school at sports. I'd like to introduce it here in order to prevent another incident like the one that occurred yesterday."

"It's the first time anything that drastic has happened," Julie protested.

"Let's hope it's the last," Mr. Justason replied. "Although I understand some of your previous games against St. Croix have been bad."

"They're our main rivals," I said.

"Yeah — they cheat and foul," said Brian. "We can't just let them get away with it."

Mr. Justason held up his hand. "Conduct yourselves with dignity and grace, the way Miss Little has taught you. I believe the Code of Conduct will reinforce Miss Little's philosophy. Are you prepared to hear it?"

No one spoke.

Mr. Justason looked right at me. "You're the captain, Shay. What do you say?"

Being captain is a funny thing. It's easy when we're on the soccer field. I tell the team what to do and they do it.

But this was different. We weren't playing a game. We were threatened with being suspended from soccer. Was I supposed to do what I thought was best, or find out what my teammates wanted, and then tell Mr. Justason?

I knew what my grandfather would say if I asked him. He was a stickler for rules, and he would tell me to obey Mr. Justason.

I looked around at my teammates, inviting them to speak.

Toby shrugged.

Brian muttered, "Whatever."

Julie nodded.

Magic lifted his hands in a hopeless gesture.

I assumed that meant they wanted to hear the code, but would they accept it? I glanced back at Miss Little, wondering how she felt about it, but her head was down.

"We're listening," I told Mr. Justason.

"Good," he said. "Rule One: Students will conduct themselves in a polite, respectful, and responsible manner at all times."

"In class?" said Brian. He sounded nervous.

"Of course in class."

"And in the community," Mrs. Stuart added.

"Rule Two," Mr. Justason went on. "Students will avoid the use of alcohol and drugs."

He looked around before continuing. "Rule Three: Students will not engage in inappropriate touching."

Julie stifled a laugh, turning it into a cough.

Mr. Justason looked up and glared at her before continuing, "Rule Four: Students will maintain an academic average of sixty-five percent."

"I'm a goner," whispered Toby.

"Rule Five concerns the way you dress ..."

"The way we *dress*?" exclaimed Julie.

"... Students will dress in clothes that are neat and tidy, and in a manner reflecting the dignity and discipline of Brunswick Valley School, which means they will avoid flamboyant colours, unseemly styles, and unnecessary personal decoration."

"What's an unnecessary personal decoration?" asked Julie.

Behind her, Linh-Mai was twisting one of the wispy red strands that dangled on each side of her face from her curly black hair with one hand, while she fingered the stud in her nose with the other. She usually wore rings in both her ears and her nose, and even had a belly button ring, which she showed us once. Her eyes flickered from Mrs. Stuart to Mr. Justason. On and off the soccer field, she was always looking around, always alert, like a skittish deer.

"I think the young lady behind you has just found two examples," said Mr. Justason.

Linh-Mai quickly put her hands in her lap.

"But what we do in class, and around the school, and in the community — that's got nothing to do with soccer," I protested.

"When you play soccer, you represent the school," said Mr. Justason. Moreover, the younger students look up to you. You need to set a good example for them."

"What if we don't dress neatly, and do all this stuff?" Brian challenged.

"You receive a demerit each time you break the rules of the Code," said Mr. Justason. "One demerit gets you suspended from half a game. Two demerits means you miss a whole game, and if you get three demerits, you're suspended from soccer for the rest of the year."

Miss Little still cupped her chin in her hands, looking down. All you could see was the long blond hair hiding her face.

3 Suspensions

I think we'd better go along with the Code," I said.

Julie agreed, tentatively. "I suppose."

"We haven't got much choice," said Toby.

We were walking home along Riverside Drive, where Julie and I are next door neighbours. Toby lives further along on the way out of town.

"We can try to be polite and respectful, right?" I said. "I mean, it's not as if we behave badly at school and get in trouble all the time." Toby — who has a habit of running off at the mouth — raised his eyebrows, and I added, "You'll just have to watch what you say."

"We'll help you," Julie offered.

"How?"

"We'll tell you to shut up."

"Great! That's very polite and respectful," said Toby.

He'd been plodding heavily a step or two behind us, as usual. Twice already we'd had to wait for him to catch his breath.

"What's the rush, guys?" Toby complained, stopping again. His hair and forehead were dripping from sweat. He took a few deep breaths, then trudged along, saying, "But even if I manage to keep quiet, my average is nowhere near sixty-five, so I'll get a demerit for that, anyway. Mr. Justason must think we're all geniuses."

"We'll help you with your work, too," I said.

"It might be too late," said Toby. "We get our marks next week."

"It's the stuff about how you dress that worries me," said Julie. She stopped, put her foot on a fire hydrant, and fingered the thin silver chain around her ankle. "I'm not taking this off."

I'd given it to her for her last birthday. Toby was the only other person who knew this.

"Keep it," he urged. "It's really cool."

"But do you suppose it's okay?" Julie asked.

"Everyone on the team thinks we should go along with the Code," I said. "I'll tell Mr. Justason tomorrow."

A week later, at the start of social studies class — the same day we were supposed to play Keswick Narrows — Mr. Justason gave us our averages. Magic had ninety-nine. Julie and I were in the eighties, and Brian surprised himself by clearing seventy.

But Toby had fifty-five.

Mr. Justason, who was walking around the class as

we looked at our marks, stopped at Toby's desk and asked, "What sort of a mark is that?"

"Well," said Toby. "It's not a prime number …"

"Don't start," I warned.

But Toby was on a rant. "… and it's one more than fifty-four, and one less than fifty-six …"

"That will do," said Mr. Justason.

"… and it's eleven times bigger than five, and five times bigger than eleven."

"Enough!" Mr. Justason snapped.

"It's forty-five less than a perfect score of one hundred — that's the bad news — but it's fifty-five more than zero, and that's the good news, because zero would be a really embarrassing average, even for me …"

Julie leaned across the aisle, punched Toby on the shoulder, and whispered, "TO-BY! SHUT UP!"

Toby jumped, curling the paper in his hands.

Mr. Justason said, "Thank you for the math lecture, Toby. Your rudeness earns you one demerit. Add that to the demerit you receive for your poor mark, and you'll be benched for this afternoon's game."

While Toby was ranting, Brian had started making drum sounds. I turned around, trying to catch his eye, but he was already in another world.

His eyes were closed and he was leaning back; his chair tilted on two legs, and his arms beat imaginary drums. "Boom-chucka-chucka —"

"Brian!" Mr. Justason suddenly roared.

"Wha …?" Brian stopped, opened his eyes, shook his head as if he was waking up, and looked around, blinking.

Mr. Justason looked grim. "You receive a demerit for disruptive behaviour. You'll be on the bench for half this afternoon's game."

At dismissal, Julie rose from her desk and stretched. As she lifted her arms over her head, her T-shirt rode up and briefly exposed her midriff.

Mr. Justason said, "Your T-shirt is inappropriately short, Julie."

Julie quickly lowered her arms, pulled her T-shirt over her jeans, and said, "Sorry, sir."

"That earns you one demerit. You'll spend half this afternoon's game on the bench with Toby and Brian."

"That's not fair!" Julie threw up her hands in disgust. "I shouldn't get a demerit because of my T-shirt style. That's an infringement of personal expression."

Ironically, Julie had learned this in a unit on human rights we'd done with Justason.

"Your right to personal expression ends where my right not to be offended begins," Mr. Justason shot back.

"How are we supposed to know where that is?" Julie demanded.

"You just found out," said Mr. Justason.

Julie opened her mouth as if she was going to answer back.

I whispered, "Leave it."

Julie waited until the principal had left the room, then roared, "Just because my T-shirt is a bit short, I'm benched for a soccer game?"

She was angry now, pointing her finger at me, "You're going to have to do something," she ordered.

"Why me?"

"You're the captain of the soccer team. Talk some sense into Mr. Justason."

"Let's see if things settle down," I pleaded. "Mr. Justason's just trying to impress Mrs. Stuart and Ms. Dugalici. Once they calm down, things will be back to normal."

"They'd better be."

"Anyway, you can't just ignore rules."

"You can stupid ones," said Julie. "What do you say, Toby?"

Toby was eating his recess snack. "Whatever," he shrugged.

"Don't get too worked up," said Julie, and flounced out of the classroom.

By the time school ended, I'd decided how to face Keswick Narrows with some of our top players missing. Julie would play the first half, and Brian the second. I'd start in goal.

Just before the game, however, I had to reorganize all over again because the twins both received demerits for giggling in the hallway.

"What was so funny?" Miss Little asked.

They looked at each other and started laughing again.

"Jessica sneezed and farted," said Jillian.

They stood in front of us like naughty children, hands behind their backs and chins down. Then they collapsed in giggles again.

"Sorry," they spluttered together.

Miss Little sighed. "Jessica, you stay out for the first half, and Jillian for the second. We'll have to manage with only eight players."

"What am I supposed to do — just sit and watch?" asked Toby.

"You can be our cheerleader," suggested Brian.

"You better give me something to cheer about, then," said Toby.

But there wasn't anything to cheer about. Despite good defense work, we lost 5–0.

After the game, Toby and Brian put away the benches, while Julie and I collected the soccer shirts for Miss Little to take home and wash. By the time we'd changed, everyone else had gone.

When Brian came out of the change room and saw the long empty hallway in front of him, he ran with his arms out, making a loud, nasal "Nnnyeeeeaaar" sound, like a plane.

Julie took off after him, shooting at him with an imaginary cannon.

Toby let out a low roar, warning, "Here comes the Big Bomber."

Brian wheeled around and faced Julie. At the same time Mr. Justason appeared from his office. Unable to stop, Julie crashed into Brian. Toby, lumbering down the hallway behind them, skidded on the tile and tumbled over, too. The three of them lay in a heap on the floor.

"What do you think you're doing?" said Mr. Justason icily.

"Having a crash landing," suggested Brian.

"Sorry," said Toby.

Julie and Brian added quickly, "Sorry, Mr. Justason."

"It's too late for sorry. You each receive two demerits, one for irresponsible behaviour and another for disrespectful conduct."

He marched back into his office.

Outside school, Toby said suddenly, "I've got four demerits! I'm finished soccer for the year."

Julie gasped, "I've got three. I'm finished, too."

"And me," Brian groaned.

"This is ridiculous," Julie fumed. "We have three players on the bench and we're supposed to play Westfield Ridge next week. Who knows how many will be suspended by then?"

She looked expectantly at me.

"I'll talk to Mr. Justason tomorrow," I promised.

Before I confronted Mr. Justason the next day, I

decided to talk to Miss Little. I got the chance when Julie and I went to the library for Book Club, where we help little kids with their reading. My reading buddy was absent, so while Julie read with her partner, I went in search of Miss Little.

Brunswick Valley School is small. The primary wing and the elementary wing meet in an L-shape, with the playground between them. It's an old, two-storey school made of brick, and looks like a prison, with several windows bricked in to save heat. The remaining windows are painted drab yellow. I walked through the pink and green hallways — painted those colours to cheer the place up — to the primary wing, and found Miss Little in her classroom, sitting among the kindergarten kids' little chairs and tables. At first I thought she was working, but then realized she was just sitting there thinking.

She looked up and said, "Hello, Shay, dear. What can I do for you?"

Miss Little always calls us "dear." It's another of her kindergarten habits.

I was going to ask her to come with me to speak to Mr. Justason, but she looked so troubled I decided not to bother her.

"Nothing, Miss Little. Thanks."

She looked at me over the top of her big glasses. "Something must be wrong, dear, or you wouldn't be standing there so awkwardly."

"Julie, Toby and Brian are all suspended from soccer," I blurted out.

"Mr. Justason told me."

"So the team is down to eight players."

Miss Little shook her head. "Seven. Linh-Mai received a demerit this morning."

"We can't play Westfield Ridge with only seven on the team," I said. "Can't we bring in some new players?"

"League rules say that if the school suspends a student from soccer, that player cannot be replaced.

"Could we talk to Mr. Justason, and ask him to ease up on the Code of Conduct?" I said desperately.

"We can try. Let's go now."

As we approached Mr. Justason's office, we heard voices through the half-closed door.

"How is the Drive for Discipline going?"

I recognized Mrs. Stuart's voice.

"I've started by making an example of the soccer players," Mr. Justason answered. "They're popular in the school; once word gets around that they are being disciplined, all the other students will fall into line."

"Excellent," said Mrs. Stuart.

"We can't eavesdrop," Miss Little whispered, leading me away. "Besides, I don't think there's much point in talking to Mr. Justason right now, do you? I'll try another day."

4 Cemetery Road

At home that evening, Grandad asked, "How's soccer?"

"Good," I lied.

I didn't want him to know about players getting suspended. I knew that if I grumbled about the Code he'd tell me "Rules are rules."

I've lived with Grandad on Riverside Drive for as long as I can remember. He's always been strict about being in at a certain time, getting homework done, being polite to everyone, and obeying teachers. When I sometimes accidentally break the rules, he doesn't get mad. I just know he's really disappointed in me, so I always try to obey them.

Through the window I saw Julie and Mrs. Barry cutting across the path Grandad had made between our houses. Julie pointed to the soccer ball she was holding.

I turned to Grandad and started, "Julie and I are going to play …"

In the few minutes I'd been thinking about Grandad and rules, he'd dozed off. He'd told me earlier he was feeling tired. Sometimes he has what he calls "the old heart trouble." He always says it's nothing serious, although he has to go to the doctor every six months for a check up. I peered more closely at him, and decided he was all right.

I tiptoed outside.

"Want to play soccer?" Julie asked.

"Take your ball down to the Back Field," said Mrs. Barry. "After I sweep the shop, I'll look in on your grandad, Shay, and tell him where you are."

Grandad ran a little flower shop in a converted garage beside our house, and Mrs. Barry helped him with it.

At the school playing field — we call it the Back Field because it's back behind the school — I went in goal so that Julie could practice shooting. She'd only taken two shots when Mrs. Paul, one of the custodians, hurried down from the school.

"You're not allowed to play on the Back Field," she called. "Mr. Justason says students may only play soccer on school grounds under the coach's supervision. Sorry, dear."

I couldn't believe it. Not only were we suspended from playing for the school, we were also suspended from playing *at* the school.

"Let's keep playing," said Julie. "I don't care if Mr.

Justason gets mad. What's he going to do — stop me from ever kicking a ball again?"

"It won't just be you he's mad at," I pointed out. "Mrs. Paul will be in trouble, too, for not stopping you. Let's kick the ball around in the back road. You can slam it at me. Pretend I'm Mr. Justason."

We went out into the back road, which goes beside the Back Field on the side opposite the school, but quickly gave up because there was too much traffic. We went around the corner to Portage Street, but there were too many parked cars.

"Let's try the cemetery footpath," I suggested.

We set off on the footpath that went through the cemetery between Portage and Main. I thought we could at least dribble the ball along, but there were too many people strolling there.

Julie grumbled, "We can't play in your driveway because your grandad's asleep, and we can't play in mine because of Little Sis, and I'm not allowed to play on the Back Field, and the roads are too busy, and the footpath's too crowded ..."

"Let's try this way," I said, pointing towards the back of the cemetery, where it was bordered by wooded hills.

We left the main footpath and followed a muddy trail through the graves. We'd never been this way before. The trail took us up and over a steep, grassy bank.

"Look, it's a secret road," said Julie.

"Yeah — the old Cemetery Road — what's left of it, anyway," I guessed.

We played soccer there until it started to get dark. First Julie thundered shots at me. Then we played a one-on-one scrimmage, with twigs stuck in the ground at each end of the Cemetery Road as our goals.

As we left, I said, "This is a good place to play soccer. Let's get Toby and Brian down here tomorrow. We'll play two on two. It'll be like a secret soccer club for kids suspended from playing at school."

"You're not suspended," Julie pointed out.

"It's only a matter of time," I said.

Even as I spoke, I wasn't sure whether it would be just a matter of time. I didn't want to disappoint Grandad by breaking Mr. Justason's rules, even if I didn't agree with them, and especially I didn't want to get suspended from playing soccer. Grandad had been a famous goalkeeper when he was young, and he often reminisced about it. A faded photograph of his old soccer team hung in the flower shop, and I liked to find him in the back row, in his green goalkeeper's sweater. He always wanted to hear all about my games, and I knew he'd be disappointed if I wasn't allowed to play.

It felt strange that I was still on the team when Julie, Toby and Brian were all suspended. I felt like a traitor to my friends — as if I was somehow betraying them, instead of betraying Grandad.

5 Traitor

The next morning found us meeting with Miss Little to discuss how we'd play Westfield Ridge with only seven on the team.

"Let's try an all-out attack at the start," I suggested. "They won't expect that, so maybe we can grab a quick goal and try to hang on to the lead."

"Let's have Jillian and Jessica play as forwards until — Has anyone seen the twins?" Miss Little asked.

At that moment Jillian and Jessica entered the cafeteria, heads down.

"Oh no!" I said.

They nodded.

"What did you get demerits for?" Miss Little asked.

"We failed a math test," said Jessica. "Even if we got perfect full marks on the next test, our average would still be below sixty-five."

"The test wasn't fair," Jillian added. "Everyone failed."

"Did you study for it?" Miss Little asked.

The twins looked at each other.

"I did," said Jessica.

"I didn't," Jillian admitted.

Miss Little looked discouraged. "Hmmm."

"Sorry, Miss Little," they said in unison.

Miss Little put her elbows on the table and briefly rested her chin in her hands, covering her face. Then she looked up and said, "We can't play with only five players. I'll call the league and report that we're dropping out for this year. Sorry, children. We did our best. Those of you still allowed to play can scrimmage. That's Shay, Flip, Quan, Magic and Brandon."

Flip and Quan glanced at one other. "We got demerits this morning, too," said Quan. "I got one for swearing when I banged my knee on my desk."

"And I got one for this," said Flip. She lifted her sweater to reveal a tank top. "Next time I'll keep my sweater on, but I was so hot after recess."

Miss Little slowly shook her head. "Then we'll have a scrimmage with just Shay, Magic and Brandon. The rest of you can watch."

She walked quickly from the cafeteria.

Julie, Toby, Brian and I lingered after the others had gone.

"What are we going to do now?" asked Brian.

"Why are you looking at me?" I said, as they turned their heads in my direction.

"You're the captain," said Toby.

"There's hardly a team left to be captain of."

You're still the captain," Brian insisted.

"I told you — you're going to have to lead a mutiny to protest the Code of Conduct," said Julie.

"Yeah — or a sit in," Brian said.

"Or a protest march," Toby added.

I rolled my eyes. "It wouldn't help. It'd just make things worse. We'd get even more demerits."

"You haven't got any demerits," Brian pointed out. "You're the only one."

"Magic and Brandon haven't got any, either."

"They don't count. They never do anything wrong."

"Let's just try not to break any more rules," I pleaded. "Then things will calm down, and Mr. Justason and Mrs. Stuart and Ms. Dugalici will forget about it and we'll be able to play soccer again."

"It's all right for you to say that," said Brian. "You *can* play soccer. We're suspended from all games, and we can't even practice on the Back Field. We've got nowhere to play."

"What about the Cemetery Road?" I suggested.

I arrived first at our secret soccer field that night. Julie had to babysit, but said she'd come later.

While I waited, I climbed up the bank towards the woods. At the top of the slope, I sat under a big maple tree and leaned my head back against the trunk, thinking about the Code of Conduct.

Being captain of the soccer team was important to me. It meant the others looked to me for a lead. But where the Code of Conduct was concerned, my lead wasn't working. I'd said we should simply be careful and try not to break the rules, but already Julie, Toby and Brian were suspended for the year, another five players were on their way to being suspended, and Miss Little had withdrawn the team from the league. Not only had my lead been a failure, but I was also beginning to wonder whether I had suggested going along with the rules because I really thought it was the best thing to do, or because I was simply afraid of breaking the rules and upsetting Grandad.

I'd thought of talking to him about it, but I was afraid he'd find out what was going on, and I remembered what he'd said the one time I'd deliberately broken the rules at school. It had been when I was in Grade 1, and I'd refused to change into my indoor shoes when I entered the classroom because they had flowers on, and the other kids teased me about them. I didn't want to tell Grandad that because he'd bought them for me for my birthday, so I just refused to wear them. After a few days of this, the teacher called Grandad.

When I got home that day, he said, "Rules are rules." I remember saying I thought having to change shoes was a silly rule, and Grandad saying it was a rule all the same. Then I sulked and said, "I don't like rules," and Grandad said, "Neither did your father. Don't end up like him."

I didn't understand what he meant by that until years later, but I knew he was serious, and from then on, although I still got teased, I obeyed the rule. Now, although I hadn't broken any of the rules in the Code of Conduct, I still didn't want Grandad to hear about the brawl with St. Croix, because I knew he'd be disappointed with my part in it.

"Ahoy there," boomed through the trees, interrupting my thoughts. "Anyone around?"

It was Toby, at the foot of the bank.

I looked down. A few leaves had already started to fall and through a gap in the foliage the evening sun was shining like a golden spotlight illuminating the length of our Cemetery Road soccer field.

I stood so Toby could see me. "Hey, Big T."

As I ran down the slope to join him, Brian appeared over the other bank, followed by Julie, Linh-Mai and the twins.

We stuck branches in the ground for goals and played girls against boys, then had a penalty shootout until it started to get dark.

When we met after school the next day, Brian brought Flip and Quan, who had received demerits for play-fighting during recess.

"Now we're both suspended from soccer for the rest of the year," shrugged Quan.

"So I brought them along," said Brian.

"To the secret club," said Julie.

"Are we a club?" asked Jillian.

"We're a secret club for suspended soccer players," I said.

"You can't be a member then," said Brian.

"It was my idea to play here!"

"But you're not suspended. You don't break rules. You haven't even got one demerit," Brian challenged.

As I walked home with Julie after our game, I was still thinking about what Brian had said. In a way, I felt like a traitor to my friends, because I hadn't been suspended from soccer yet. I was torn between betraying my friends and letting down Grandad.

6 Betrayal

In the end, I didn't have to make a choice about whom to betray. The choice was made for me.

And I betrayed Grandad.

Julie, Toby and I were heading to the cafeteria when Julie asked how my grandad was feeling. The night before he'd complained of being tired and dizzy, and I'd called Julie's mom, who used to be a nurse.

"He keeps saying he's all right, but I'm not sure," I told Julie.

"Mom will keep an eye on him," said Julie.

"I know. But still —" I said nervously.

Julie gave me a reassuring hug. "He'll be all right."

Miss Little, on duty at the end of the hallway, called, "No touching, children."

Mr. Justason emerged from his office. "What was that? Who's doing the touching, Miss Little?" There was an uncomfortable pause.

"Nobody," Miss Little said. "It was only a quick hug."

"By whom?" he demanded.

Miss Little looked apologetically at us. "Julie and Shay."

"That's inappropriate," Justason said sternly. "Both of you get demerits."

"You can't give me a demerit," Julie shot back. "I'm suspended from soccer already."

"In that case …" said Mr. Justason, "I'll … I'll carry your demerits into next year. You're benched for half the first game of next year."

"Hey, everybody," Toby wisecracked, "Julie has a demerit credit."

"That's a demerit for you, too," the principal replied savagely.

Toby and Julie laughed.

"I suggest the two of you take a lesson from Shay on how to accept reprimands," finished Mr. Justason icily.

His glance fell to Julie's feet as he turned towards his office. "You're wearing a bracelet on your ankle. That's unnecessary personal decoration. Get rid of it."

He marched into his office.

"No way," breathed Julie.

When I started to follow Mr. Justason, Julie tried to stop me. She knew that I was about to do something extreme. She knew it took a lot for me to reach my limit sometimes, but when I did, I went all out. That's what happened in the game with St. Croix, when I attacked Hawler.

42

"That wasn't fair," I blurted out at Mr. Justason. "What's wrong with Julie hugging me? She was just trying to ... show support about Grandad."

"Touching is inappropriate in school," lectured the principal. What your Grandad allows at home is your business, but I will not tolerate that behaviour here."

And that's when I betrayed Grandad.

"If I said that was stupid, would that cost me a demerit for being disrespectful?"

"Yes, of course."

"And if I said the Code of Conduct sucks ..."

"That would be two more demerits — for rudeness and for using inappropriate language."

"Getting a demerit for a hug is stupid and the Code of Conduct sucks."

"You're suspended from soccer for the rest of the year," said Mr. Justason, quietly and tight-lipped.

I stalked out and found Miss Little in the hallway.

"I'll try talking to Mr. Justason again," she whispered.

"It won't do any good," I muttered.

"I'll try, anyway, and if Mr. Justason won't listen, then perhaps I'll try someone else." She marched into the principal's office.

Julie and Toby were waiting for me in the cafeteria. Brian was there, too.

"What happened?" said Julie.

"I told Mr. Justason that you and me getting a demerit for inappropriate touching was stupid, and that you getting a demerit for wearing a little ankle bracelet wasn't fair, and that the Code of Conduct sucked, and now I'm suspended from soccer for the year."

"Congratulations," said Brian.

"I knew you were going to do something like that," said Julie. She put her hand on my arm. "Are you calmed down yet?"

"Not until I've broken every rule in the Code of Conduct," I said.

As we walked home after our next game at the Cemetery Road, Brian said, "But why do you have to break every rule?"

"Because if I'm going to break one rule, I'm going to break them all," I said.

"It's the way he is," said Julie.

"Will it do any good?" Toby wondered.

"It won't make Mr. Justason change his mind about the Code of Conduct, but that's not the point. The point is — to make a statement. Are you with me?"

"We've broken most of the rules already," said Brian. "What's left?"

"There's the rule about academic average, but that's easy to break. All we have to do is flunk a couple of tests."

"I can manage that," Brian commented.

"I've flunked already," Toby said proudly. "So what's next?"

"Not much," I admitted. "We've all behaved irresponsibly and disrespectfully."

"And I got a demerit for dressing inappropriately, just because my stomach was showing for half a second when I stretched," said Julie. She added thoughtfully, "Linh-Mai got one, too, because of her coloured hair and her rings. How come it's just the girls who get demerits for dressing inappropriately?"

"We'll change that," I said.

That's how Toby, Brian and I came to wear nose rings and show our stomachs at school the next day. We folded our tee shirts inside themselves to bare our stomachs, and borrowed nose rings from Linh-Mai.

"Make sure you wash them before you give them back," she threatened.

We got ready in the classroom before school started. Julie and Linh-Mai helped us fix our nose rings — they were clip on ones — and we'd just tucked our T-shirts up inside themselves when Ms. Watkins walked in for French. She looked at us and burst out laughing. At recess we paraded up and down the hallway in front of Mr. Justason's office until he saw us. I don't know whether he gave us demerits. That wasn't the point of doing it.

Toby asked, "Can I be exempted from inappropriate touching?" Julie, Toby and I were looking after the flower shop for Grandad on Saturday morning.

"Why?" I said.

Toby flushed. "I'll be embarrassed."

"We'll do it with you," I offered. "We got demerits for a little hug; let's break the rule properly this time."

"I know," said Julie. "Let's go around kissing everybody! Justason will love that."

"Bleccch!" said Toby.

We had the "kiss-in" two days later at lunch time in the cafeteria when Mr. Justason was on duty. Julie made sure he watched as she hugged and kissed me. I gave her a quick one back.

"Now you, Brian," Julie urged.

Brian turned to Jillian, who was sitting beside him, and asked, "Can I kiss you?"

Jillian recoiled in horror. "I'd sooner stick my face in a puddle of cold vomit."

"Is that a no?" said Brian.

"Just kidding," said Jillian. She grabbed him and kissed him, and he kissed her back.

Mr. Justason, watching us, just shook his head.

"Are you joining the kiss-in?" Julie asked Toby.

"Later."

But at the end of the day, Toby still hadn't kissed anyone.

"What's the problem?" I asked.

"Don't know how to," Toby mumbled.

★ ★ ★

"What do you mean — you don't know how? You just stick your lips on someone's face. It's easy." Toby had been hard to steer onto the kissing topic the whole walk home from school.

"Easy for you to say. You've done it."

"You must have kissed your mom at least."

"We're not a kissing family. We're more of a hugging and punching family. Mom hugs me, and Conrad punches me — not hard, just lightly, usually on the shoulder. It's what they do instead of kissing me, I think."

"Didn't your mom ever kiss you good night when you were little?"

"No."

"What did she do, then? I'm sure she didn't just tuck you in and leave you."

Toby looked sheepish.

"Well?" I prompted.

"She hugged me."

"And?"

"And said, 'Silly billy teepums, time to go to sleepums.'"

I shook my head. "No wonder you're weird."

"I thought I could find out how to do it from my *How Girls and Boys Are Different* book. There's all kinds of stuff in there, but nothing about kissing. Then I looked up kissing in the dictionary, and all it says is something about touching lips."

"You can practice when we get home — on a cushion."

"I'll suffocate."

"Okay, a balloon. I've got some left over from Grandad's birthday."

"It might burst. It could blow my head off."

"Girls know more about kissing than boys," I said. "We'll ask Julie to help."

Toby blushed.

When Julie joined us later, I said, "Toby's got a problem."

"Only one?" said Julie.

"Ha, ha," said Toby.

"He wants to know how to kiss," I said. "He needs someone to practice on."

Julie looked at Toby. "Someone like me, I suppose."

"Can you show him how?" I pleaded.

"You better be careful, Toby," she warned. "I don't want you slobbering all over my face. Okay. Close your eyes."

Toby closed his eyes.

"Put your lips together and push them a little bit forward."

Toby obeyed again.

Julie crossed silently to him, kissed him, and said, "That's all there is to it."

"That's easy," he said.

Conrad arrived to visit Grandad and give Toby a

ride home. He came straight in the house and called, "Anyone home?"

I called, "Grandad's watching television. We're up here."

"Hi, guys," Conrad called. "What are you doing?"

"Toby's kissing Julie," I said.

"That boy's out of control," Conrad muttered.

★ ★ ★

The next day, they kissed in the cafeteria, while the rest of us clapped. Toby thanked Julie for helping him.

"How was it?" he asked.

"Yours was lovely …" said Julie.

Toby blushed.

"How was mine?" she pressed.

Toby put his hands over his heart and said, "It was like being kissed by a cloud."

Julie stuck her finger down her throat and pretended she was going to throw up. Then she turned to me. "Now what rule do we have to break?"

"Next — we do drugs," I said.

7 Ice

But I don't do drugs," said Toby.

"I don't know anything about drugs and I don't want to," Julie added firmly.

"Neither do I," I admitted. "But the Code says no drugs, so if we're going to break every rule, we have to find some. I know who to ask."

"Who?" asked Toby.

"Ice," I said.

Ice was already in Grade 6 when we started kindergarten. Now he was at the high school. I knew him — sort of — because just after I'd started kindergarten, I got lost on my way to class and ended up down by the gym, where the Grade 6 students used to hang out in the changing rooms. One of them came out and said, "There's a baby in the hallway." Another looked out and said, "Bring him in here. Give him a smoke." One took my hand and started to lead me into the changing rooms when Ice came out and said,

"Quit it." They let me go immediately. Ice bent down to me and said, "I guess you're looking for Miss Little's room. Go down there and turn right — you know which is your right? — and you'll see it in front of you." He watched me walk uncertainly back down the hallway. When I reached the place he'd told me to turn right, I looked back, and he gave an encouraging nod. After that, although we never spoke, whenever he saw me he'd give a tiny wink of his eye. When he went to high school I saw him only occasionally, around the town, or watching our soccer games, and he was always with a bunch of older students. But we still acknowledged one another, he by lifting his index finger and carving a small arc in the air, me with a little nod of my head. I wouldn't say we were friends — but it was a kind of acquaintance.

"How do you know Ice has drugs?" asked Toby.

"Everybody knows," I said.

Julie nodded agreement.

"How do you know where to find him?" Toby persisted.

"Everybody knows that, too," I said.

Julie nodded again.

"Everybody except me, I guess," said Toby.

It was two days after the kiss-in and we were on Main Street, walking home from school. I led the way as we cut down the alley between Valley Hardware and the Main Street Convenience to Main Street Parallel, a dirt road that runs behind the businesses on Main Street. Ice was on the other side of the road, at the edge of a patch of dense, scrubby woods. He was huddled with two high school students, and they were smoking. I beckoned to him. He said something to his friends and they laughed. He sauntered over. His jeans and his sweat shirt and his long trench coat were black, and his long, wild, curly hair was black, too. It hung over his eyes. His face was thin and carved inwards under his cheek bones.

He sucked on his cigarette, threw it on the ground, and trod on it. "What's up, guys?"

His voice was low and raspy.

I took a deep breath. "Do you have any drugs?"

He looked us over and grunted, "What sort of drugs?"

"Any sort."

"Dextromethorpham?"

I nodded. "Sounds good."

"That's cough medicine."

"Oh."

"You want something a little stronger? This stuff's good."

He produced a small plastic container and shook some white powder from it into the palm of his hand. "Try some." He held his hand towards Toby.

Toby looked from the powder to Ice. "Do I lick it or sniff it?"

Ice laughed. "You can do what you like with it but it won't give you much of a buzz. It's baby powder. I use it to stop my collar chafing." He rubbed it on his neck and went on, "I'd guess you guys are new to the drug scene."

"We've used plenty of drugs," Julie retorted quickly.

"Like what, darling?" Ice challenged.

"Don't call me darling," she snapped.

"What do you want me to call you — sweetheart?"

Julie snorted, folded her arms, and looked away.

Ice laughed again. "Look — I know what you're doing. You're breaking all the rules — right? We heard about it up at the high school, and it's cool. Of course, all your little rebellion is going to get you is a load of trouble, but it's cool. Now, if you want to break the rule about drugs, there's an easier way than getting into any stupid bad stuff."

"What easier way?" I said.

"Like just smoke a cigarette — a regular cigarette — and swig a beer. Nicotine and alcohol are drugs."

"I hadn't thought of that," I admitted.

"How were you planning to let the principal know you were doing the drugs thing?" Ice went on. "I suppose you were going to take the stuff down to the playground and do it there."

"Well ..." I started.

"That'd be really smart. I'll do something else for you. I'll put the word around you've been drinking and smoking, so it gets back to your school."

"How will you do that?"

"Leave it to me."

"But we'll still have to do it."

"I understand."

He fished in the pockets of his trench coat and produced a cigarette and matches. He lit the cigarette. "Here. Take one puff each and don't inhale. I don't want you puking over me."

We passed the cigarette around. When it was my turn I sucked briefly, and quickly released the smoke. I felt like a dirty stovepipe.

Ice said, "Smoking's a stupid, dirty habit."

"So why do you do it?" Julie challenged.

"Don't ask, darling," he growled.

"Don't call me darling," she snapped.

Ice chuckled and produced a can of beer from his trench coat — I wondered what else he had in his pockets — and said, "You'd better do your drinking here, too."

He flipped it open and ordered, "One mouthful each. Leave the rest for me."

I was last to take a swig. It tasted like flat pop mixed with dirt.

I passed the can back to Ice and said, "What do we owe you?"

"You've given me a laugh. That's enough."

We didn't speak all the way home.

I don't know how Ice did it, but Mr. Justason had learned about our latest rule breaking by the following morning. Before first class even started his voice on the intercom ordered Toby, Julie and me to report to the office, where he told us he'd heard about our party of the night before.

"Party?" I said.

"Your party on Main Street Parallel, where drink and drugs were consumed," he said.

"Oh," I said. "That party."

Mr. Justason consulted a paper on his desk. "With the demerits you've already accumulated you won't be playing soccer for a long time." He looked steadily at us. "There can't be any more rules for you to break."

8 Wanderers

The next time we played on the Cemetery Road, Julie said wistfully, "This is fun — but I wish we could have a real game, on a real soccer field."

We were sitting on the bank, taking a break from our scrimmage.

"We've got nearly the whole team here," Brian pointed out. "All we need is someone to play against."

"All the schools have a team," said Julie. "We're just not allowed to play against them."

"Who says?" I asked.

"Justason and Dugalici," said Julie.

"They said we're not allowed to play at school — nothing about playing against other schools."

"But we're not a school team," said Brian.

"And we'd have to be in the league, so the schools would have time to schedule games," Julie added.

"So let's join the league!" I said.

We looked at one another. Brian raised his eyebrows.

"Why not?" I urged.

"Only one problem," Julie said. "We would have to contact the league people — we'd need an adult for it to sound right."

"Or someone who sounds like an adult," I said. "Someone who's not too concerned with rules ... Someone who's out of the mainstream ..."

★ ★ ★

"You've got to be kidding," said Ice.

Julie and I had found him on Main Street Parallel. He was by himself, smoking on the edge of the woods.

"All you have to do is use an adult voice and act grown up ..." I pleaded.

"I am grown up."

"Pretend you're our soccer coach ..." Julie added.

"And ask if our soccer team can join the league for the rest of this season," I finished.

"What's in it for me?"

"We'll owe you," I offered.

"You bet you will."

I produced a flyer that the league had sent to schools at the beginning of the season and pointed to the bottom of the page. "There's the person to contact — Charles Finch, President. You can call from my house."

"I'll do the dirty deed now," said Ice. He searched in his pockets for a small, red cellphone. He punched in the number at the bottom of the page, and spoke in a deeper voice than usual. "Good afternoon, Mr. Finch … This is Ice … er … Mr. Ice … Just call me Ice … I'd like my soccer team to play in the league … Yes, I know it's late in the season … Yes, my players would be happy to do that … What school? Oh … ah … Cemetery Road School …"

I looked at Julie and whispered, "Cemetery Road School?"

Ice went on, "It's a small private school in Brunswick Valley … Recently started playing soccer … The school address is … er … Cemetery Road, Brunswick Valley … Thank you, Mr. Finch. We appreciate your cooperation."

He folded his cellphone away.

"Well?" I prompted.

"You're in the league," said Ice.

"Thank you," Julie smiled. "That was brilliant."

"Mr. Finch said there was a vacancy in the league because one school has dropped out …"

"That'd be Brunswick Valley," I said.

"… But you'd have to play all your games away because he didn't want to ask the other schools to travel when he's just told them they won't have to."

"That's good, because we don't have a field," I said.

"That's not all," Ice added. "The other teams will play twice as many games — home and away. Mr. Finch said that was the only way you could join."

"How does a school contact us to arrange a game?" I said. "They'll need a telephone number."

"They've got one," said Ice. "Finch has call display. He said he'd recorded my number and that they would be calling to arrange the games. So I guess I'll be getting the calls."

"You'll be our manager," said Julie, grinning.

"You really owe me," Ice threatened.

Ice was waiting at the school gate the next day.

"You've got a game on Friday," he said. "Their coach called last night. You're playing Keswick Narrows. How are you going to get there?"

"I hadn't thought of that," I admitted.

Keswick Narrows is a few kilometers upriver. The houses there are bigger than the ones in Brunswick Valley. They all have huge lawns and lots of flowers.

"Figures," Ice scoffed. "I suppose you're expecting me to help out again."

"Can you?" I said hopefully.

"I've got a friend with a van," Ice began.

"Our parents wouldn't want us riding in a stranger's van," I said doubtfully.

"But you know me, and it's my friend who has the van, so it's not really a stranger's van."

"Is it ... safe?"

"He has a licence to drive groups around, and it's covered for insurance and everything, if that's what you mean. He even takes his church youth club on trips. You'd just have to give him gas money."

I told the team about the game when we met at the Cemetery Road after supper. Keswick Narrows was far enough away that we shouldn't be recognized. How would Justason and the others react if they knew we were playing in the league? How would Mr. Finch react if he heard about our deception? Surely they would disapprove.

"Can we have a name for our team?" said Toby. "'Cemetery Road' is a bit sad."

"Well — since we have to wander around for games," I said thoughtfully, "we could call ourselves the Wanderers — the Cemetery Road Wanderers."

It was also like the name of the club Grandad had played for when he was a goalkeeper — the Newcastle Wanderers. Everyone seemed pleased with the name.

In the middle of our meeting, Ice sauntered down the slope from the woods on the edge of the cemetery.

"Just checking up on my team," said Ice. "Your van will be at the Portage Street gate right after school tomorrow. Now I'm wondering about your tactics.

I turned to Ice. "What do you mean?"

"By the look of it you've got only nine players, and last time I checked there were eleven on a soccer team, which means Keswick Narrows is going to have a two-man advantage — excuse me, darlings, I mean a *two-person* advantage."

"We'll concentrate on defence, and hope we

can get a breakaway goal," I said.

"And who's going to get your breakaway goals?"

I looked around our team. Our best strikers were Magic and Brandon, the only two who hadn't joined the Wanderers.

"I like playing fullback best, but I can score," Toby offered.

"With only nine players, you can't just stay up front, and you won't be able to chase up and down the field for ninety minutes, will you?" said Ice.

Toby glanced down at his chunky frame and shook his head. "Guess not."

"You'll do more good staying back. The defence will need your strength and experience."

Toby looked up, brightening.

"So how do you think we should play?" Julie asked.

"I'd use the Thin Red Line tactic," said Ice, sitting on a gravestone.

We clustered around him.

"Thin Red Line?" I queried.

"It's a military expression — comes from the Crimean War — meaning *brave defending against overwhelming odds*," Ice explained. "This is how it works: after kickoff everyone lines up across the field — all except the goalie — on the edge of the penalty area. Try to avoid too much space between you so their players can't run through."

"You mean stand in a line right across the field?" I said. "They'll laugh at us."

"That's right. And with any luck they'll forget how to play soccer — for a while. They'll fuss around waiting for a turn to run at your single line of defence, and that's when your fastest player —"

"Julie," I supplied.

"… That's when you, darling …" said Ice, looking at Julie.

"Don't call me darling," said Julie, through clenched teeth.

"… That's when you, sweet pea," Ice went on, unabashed, "… take off up the field. At the same time your best passer —"

"Shay," said Brian.

"… lobs the ball over the opposition to Julie, who waltzes it around their goalie, who'll be the only one left to beat."

"I'd be offside," Julie pointed out.

"You can't be offside in your own half, so you just have to make sure you don't cross the halfway line before you get Shay's pass."

"How do you know so much about soccer?" said Julie.

"From stuff I've heard," said Ice, and went on quickly. "Have you thought about uniforms?" He looked at me. "You'd better make it white shirts — everyone's got a white shirt of some kind — and black shorts, or as near white and black as you can get."

He added, "You know, this is crazy. You're playing under false pretences, and you're going to get caught. Even if by some miracle you didn't, the other teams play twice as many games as you, so you're bound to finish bottom of the league. Are you sure it's worth it?"

"I don't know," I admitted. "What do you say?"

"I think it's a blast," said Ice.

"So why are you telling me all this?"

"Just don't want you guys getting disappointed," Ice mumbled.

9 Thin Red Line

Julie and I ran home to change after school on Friday. I threw on soccer clothes, shouted into the flower shop, "I'm playing soccer, Grandad," and found Julie already waiting at the end of her driveway. We met the others and took the footpath across to the Portage Street gate. A van was pulled over, its hood propped open.

"Is that it?" said Linh-Mai.

It was a long cargo van, with windows cut in the sides and painted in swirling stripes of black and white, as if it was about to go on safari. Lettering on the side proclaimed Valley Full Gospel Assembly, and on the back, Exotic Bar Excursions Ltd.

Ice was standing beside the van.

"Are you coming with us?" I asked.

"You don't think I'd work out your strategy and not come, do you?" he retorted. He pointed to the van. "What do you think?"

The bottom was rusty, and parts of the body had

been filled with fiberglass and repainted. The rear fender was hanging down at one side. One window was cracked, and duct tape covered the other where there had once been glass.

"Does it go?" said Toby.

"Oh — it goes," said Ice. "Grease — that's him under the hood — is the best mechanic in town."

I pointed to the lettering. "What are these names?"

"Some of the clubs Grease drives for have their name on the van," Ice explained.

Grease emerged from under the hood and slammed it shut. He wore an oil-smeared yellow vest and baggy camouflage pants which came down to the top of his ankles, exposing his big boots. A chain dangled from his belt and a tiny silver cross pierced his right eyebrow. His head was shaved except for a column of spiked green hair down the centre, and his nose bent to one side. A long scar across his right cheek looked pink against his pale skin.

"This is Grease," said Ice. "He doesn't say much — do you, Grease?"

Grease shook his head.

"Here's money for gas," I said, handing him the $9.34 I'd collected from the team. He stuffed it in his pocket without looking at it. "Is that enough?" I asked.

He nodded.

"How did Grease get the scar?" I whispered to Ice as we climbed in the van.

"Looking after me," said Ice.

We spread ourselves along the four rows of seats. They were covered in a smooth leopard-skin fabric. The same fabric covered the sides and roof of the van. A pair of wooly dice hung from the rear view mirror.

Ice sat in the front with Grease and advised, "Keep it clean. Grease doesn't like a mess — do you, Grease?"

Grease shook his head and started the van. The engine ran so smoothly we could hardly hear it.

Keswick Narrows Memorial School consisted of four low white buildings, joined by glass walkways to a higher white building in the centre.

"Is it a school or a space station?" said Ice.

Grease drove us through landscaped grounds and stopped at the playing field beside the buildings where the Keswick Narrows players were warming up.

I looked from their green and yellow uniforms to our team outfits as we climbed from the van. We'd all found a white shirt of some kind, although they were in a variety of styles. Quan had a long sleeve dress shirt with frills down the front — he said he'd borrowed it from his older brother — while Brian wore a sleeveless vest and Toby a white T-shirt with "Drink More Beer" on the front. Most of us had black or gray shorts, and all of us had long white or black soccer socks, except the twins and Flip. They had short socks in brilliant colours: Jillian bright yellow, Jessica hot pink, and Flip lime green.

Ice, seeing them, commented, "Nice hoofs, dar-lings."

Julie looked the part in her white soccer shirt, black shorts and long white soccer socks.

"You look professional," said Toby, admiringly.

"You, too, Big T," said Julie. "You look like David Beckham."

Toby always claimed he and the English soccer star were twins because they both had short, spiky blonde hair. Toby said he wasn't copying David Beckham. It was David Beckham who was copying him. The trou-ble was, David Beckham seemed to change his hair style every week and there was no way Toby could keep up. Besides, Mr. Beckham didn't have a chunky build like Toby.

"We look as if we're going to play for England, in our black and white outfits," Toby commented.

The home coach, who wore a track suit that matched his team's colours, jogged across to introduce himself, "I'm Mr. Parsons. Welcome to Keswick Nar-rows Memorial School. Where's your coach?"

"That'd be me," said Ice.

"You're very young to be a coach."

"I'm a coach-in-training."

"And who's this?" Mr. Parsons said, looking nerv-ously at Grease, who had opened the hood and was inspecting the engine again.

"He's my assistant," said Ice.

As we prepared to take the field, Mr. Parsons said, "I think we've played against some of your team before."

"Could be," said Ice. "Some of our students are recent transfers to Cemetery Road." He turned quickly and clapped his hands. "Hurry up. Get on the field."

When we won the toss, I told the referee we'd take the kick off.

The opposing players took their positions. The Wanderers, all except me, stood in a line across the field on the edge of the penalty area, with only Brian in goal behind them. I stood at the centre spot.

"What's going on?" said the referee.

"We're taking the kickoff," I said.

"But you've only got nine players. You can't start without a full team."

I looked at Ice.

He called to the referee, "The rules say a team must have at least seven players and not more than eleven, so nine is okay."

"Is that all right with you?" the referee asked the Keswick Narrows coach.

Mr. Parsons nodded. "I guess so."

"It doesn't matter if it's all right with him or not," said Ice.

"Tell your team to take their positions, then," the referee told me.

"They're in them," I said.

"They can't stand in a line across the field."

"Who says?"

"It's not regular."

Ice called, "As long as all players are in their own half of the field, they can stand where they like for the kick off."

The referee looked at Coach Parsons, shrugged, and blew the whistle to start. I tapped the ball into their end and ran back to join the line. Julie was on one side of me and Toby on the other. A few students from the home school were watching and snickering at our maneuvers. Number 5 — a tall, gangly boy with thin legs — dribbled towards Toby.

When he was a metre away, Toby smiled and said, "How-de-doody, pal."

Number 5 stopped and said, "Eh?"

As the ball trickled away from his feet, Toby punted it towards the Keswick goal. The goalkeeper grabbed it and started another advance. Number 5 tried to run between Linh-Mai and Jillian, but they closed the gap. Then he tried to dribble between Julie and me. Eventually Julie took the ball and kicked it back into the Keswick Narrows end.

The spectators started a slow hand clap. I heard Number 5 grumble, "Play a proper game."

On the sideline, Ice grinned and winked.

Keswick Narrows advanced yet again.

"When I move forward — everybody move with me," I whispered to Julie and Toby. "Pass it down the line."

Number 5 kept the ball while his team stood poised to run between us. As he swung his foot to kick the ball, I moved forward, and the line moved with me, past the home players, leaving only Brian between them and the goal.

The referee whistled. "Offside."

Number 5 groaned. The slow clapping resumed, louder.

When we left the field at halftime, I overheard the Keswick Narrows players grumble among themselves. "This is like kicking the ball against a wall."

During the break, Ice said, "Take your regular positions for the start of the second half, but as soon as they take the kick off, run back and form your line. That'll keep them guessing."

Our opponents looked relieved that we were about to play a normal game. Number 5 kicked off with a flourish, making a show of passing behind him before spinning around to run upfield. He stopped and gaped when he saw us racing back into our line. He and another guy passed the ball casually between them, as if they were playing a game of monkey in the middle with me. I watched a few passes go back and forth, then leaped forward and intercepted the ball. When I looped the ball high over the Keswick players, it landed in front of Julie, who collected it just before she crossed the halfway line.

"Go, darling!" Ice shouted.

Julie ran around the goalkeeper and tapped the ball into the net. She turned, arms high, grinning.

The Keswick Narrows coach shouted, "No goal. Offside."

The referee hesitated, blew his whistle, and echoed, "Off-side!"

"I think not," called Ice. He strode onto the pitch, his open trench coat flapping behind him. He plucked a tattered book from his pocket. "Take a look at the rules. A player can't be off-side in his or her own side of the field," he said, planting his finger on the page.

The referee read and announced, "You're right. Goal — I guess."

For the next ten minutes, Keswick Narrows attacked our line ferociously, but we held firm. Then, they seemed to grow dispirited. It was a boring way to play, I'll admit. Their attacks were half-hearted, so we held onto our lead until the game ended.

The Wanderers had won their first league encounter.

We had to be careful the following week at school to keep the Wanderers a secret, despite our excitement at winning.

Toby ran into the classroom on Monday morning. "Great win!" he said breathlessly.

When I looked at him sharply he added quickly, "I mean the hockey game on TV last night."

As we left French class, Julie asked anxiously, "Do you think we can use that tactic again?"

Ms. Watkins overheard. "What tactic would that be?" she asked.

I made up some story that Julie had discovered a good chess move the night before.

Outside, in a whisper, I answered Julie's question. "We won't get away with a stunt like that again. We need goals in soccer or we're going to get badly beaten."

10 Winners

Magic and Brandon always did their work — well. They were serious, A students.

In fact, Brandon was more than quiet. He was totally silent. He hadn't spoken since kindergarten. No one knew why as far as I know. He never answered questions or took part in class discussions; he never got in trouble for talking, or using bad language, or being loud. His mission in life seemed to be to make himself invisible. In addition to never speaking, he never looked at you. His hair was dull yellow, as if the sun had bleached out all the colour, and his complexion was so pale you expected to see the face bones underneath. Despite his slight build, he was a star striker, with a mighty shot.

Magic, with his round eyes and round nose, looked a bit like a monkey. We called him 'Magic' because of the way he ghosted into scoring positions in soccer, and got straight A's in school without seeming to study.

Whenever someone asked him how he got them, he'd shrug and say something like, "I was just lucky."

At recess a few days after the game with Keswick Narrows, Magic and Brandon sat beside the dumpster, as usual, hidden from the playground. Both had Walkmans over their ears and were writing in exercise books balanced on their knees. Every now and then one would lean over and point to the other's work. After recess, while we waited in social studies class for Mr. Justason, I realised Magic and Brandon hadn't returned to class.

I whispered to Julie, "I'll bet they couldn't hear the bell because of their Walkmans. I'll get them."

Just as I stood, Mr. Justason swept into the room. Magic and Brandon hurried in behind him.

"Sorry we're late," said Magic. "We didn't hear the bell."

"You each get a demerit for being late," said Mr. Justason.

"But we've never been late before."

"And I don't expect you ever to be late again. What about you, Brandon. Would you like to apologize, too?"

Of course Brandon said nothing.

"I repeat — would you like to apologize?"

Either he'd forgotten that Brandon never spoke, or he hadn't learned that yet in the few weeks at our school.

"Very well," Mr. Justason said. "You receive two

demerits — one for being late and one for refusing to apologize."

"Brandon doesn't speak," Magic explained.

"He should have told me," Mr. Justason snapped.

Julie, Toby and I burst out laughing. Then we realized he hadn't meant it as a joke.

"That's stupid," said Magic.

He put his hands in his pockets and stared at Mr. Justason. At that instant I understood he was like me. He didn't like to break the rules — but once he started, he couldn't stop.

"That gets you another demerit," he roared.

Magic scowled and he and Brandon sauntered to their seats.

Between classes, I said to Magic, "Too bad about the soccer. Do you want to play with the Wanders?"

"The Wanderers?"

I told them about playing secretly at the Cemetery Road.

"I'm in," said Magic.

And Brandon nodded too.

Ice got off the bus from the high school as we were walking past the Main Street Convenience on the way home.

"The Westfield Ridge coach called this morning in French class," he said.

"You answered your cellphone during French?" I said incredulously.

"Sure," said Ice. "I told Mme. LaPointe, 'Je doit repond, s'il vous plait, Madame.' And she said, 'Bien, Ice.' Please take your call outside.' Anyway, the game's next week. I suppose you'd like me to arrange transport again."

"Yes, please. We'll have a full team," I said. "Magic and Brandon are playing."

"That means I won't have to think of any fancy tactics. It'll be a piece of cake."

We met on the Cemetery Road, and later found Ice and Grease listening to the van idle. Ice wore a soccer shirt under his trench coat.

"Where did you get that?" I asked.

He shrugged. "I found it in my closet. I thought I might as well look the part."

Then I noticed that the van had Cemetery Road Wanderers painted on both sides.

"How much do we owe for having our name painted on the van?" I worried.

Grease grunted and shook his head.

Ice said, "It's all part of the service."

Most of the people from Westfield Ridge work in the city, so it was quiet as we drove along. The town looked nice enough — lots of malls, subdivisions, and golf clubs where you have to wear the right clothes. Grease found a parking spot, then stood with Ice to watch the game.

Ice was right. It was an easy game. Fifteen minutes

after the start we scored our first goal. Julie robbed one of the Westfield Ridge forwards of the ball and slipped it to me. I kept it while I surveyed the field. A few seconds earlier Magic had been helping defend. Now, from the corner of my eye, I saw him drifting unhurriedly through the Westfield Ridge midfield and defence into a space on the left touchline. I swept the ball out to the wing, where Magic was already moving toward the goal. The defenders rushed to cut him off. He waited until they were close to him before pushing the ball to Brandon, whose shot was in the net before the goalkeeper could move.

We scored again when Toby cleared the ball out to the wing, where Jillian raced the length of the pitch with it before cutting the ball back to Brandon, who weaved around two defenders, then twisted and turned as the other backs swarmed frantically around him. Suddenly he straightened out and raced towards the side of the penalty area. The defenders went with him — but the ball didn't. Brandon had left it behind him for Magic, who'd been standing to one side watching Brandon's dribbling antics. Magic calmly walked the ball past the goalkeeper and into the net.

We scored twice more in the second half — one each from Brandon and Magic — and won 4–0.

Ice was scribbling on a scrap of paper as we left the field. He greeted us, "I'm figuring out points in the league table. You're gaining."

We'd started at the bottom, of course, because we hadn't played any games, while the other teams had played at least four. It was lucky for us that there had been lots of ties, with teams earning only one point instead of the three points they would have earned for a win; otherwise, we'd have been hopelessly behind.

"I got the positions from the Westfield Ridge coach," Ice went on. "You're in the middle. If you win the next game, you could be second from the top."

"Who's top?" I asked.

Ice shrugged. "St. Croix Middle School."

I groaned.

We were doing a newspaper project in Language Arts a few days later when Betsy, who sits behind Toby, said, "This doesn't look good on Brunswick Valley."

We had to discover how many times the community was mentioned in the different newspapers we'd brought from home, and how it was presented through the media.

"What have you found?" our language arts teacher, Mr. Swanson, asked.

"The headline is 'Brunswick Valley School Gives Up.'"

"What does it say?" Mr. Swanson asked.

Betsy read, "Student suspensions have forced Brunswick Valley School to drop out of the Fundy Schools Soccer League. The team has been replaced by the Cemetery Road Wanderers, from Cemetery Road

School. The Wanderers have made an impressive start, winning their first two games."

"I've never heard of Cemetery Road School," commented James.

"My cousin in Westfield Ridge played against them," said Josh. "He thought some of the players were from Brunswick Valley."

"What do you mean?" I asked nervously.

"He's seen them around."

"Well, whoever they are — they've got a good soccer team," said Michelle. "My cousin was in that game, too, and he says they were awesome."

I glanced at Julie. She caught my eye and smiled slowly.

"That's enough," said Mr. Swanson. "Time to log off your computers."

At the end of class, Brian asked Michelle, "Did your cousin say anything about the goalkeeper?"

"Why?"

"Brian," I said. "I think Julie wants you."

Julie was talking to Linh-Mai on the other side of the room.

"Just curious," Brian told Michelle.

"Brian," I said more loudly. "Julie wants you."

Michelle was deep in thought. "He did say something about the goalkeeper."

"Julie," I called. "Didn't you want Brian to help you with ... with your language arts homework?"

Julie looked up and frowned. "You think I want help from *Brian*?"

I nodded frantically, pointing surreptitiously to Brian and Michelle.

"I remember," said Michelle. "He said the goalkeeper was brilliant."

"Oh — yes," said Julie. She called, "Brian …"

"Are you sure he said brilliant?" said Brian.

"BRIAN," Julie yelled.

Brian jumped. "What?"

"Come here."

"Why?"

"I want help with my language arts homework."

"You're asking *me* for help? You must be joking."

"Come here or I'll pound you."

Brian obeyed, while I sighed with relief.

On Saturday morning, I was delivering flowers for Grandad, when Ice appeared at the end of Main Street Parallel. He'd received a call from the St. Croix coach asking when his team could play the Wanderers.

I knew we'd be recognized by St. Croix, then word would get back and it would all be over.

"What did you tell him?"

"I said we were writing exams so the game would have to wait until next week."

"Shouldn't we play Bethel Station first? At least we can get that game in before we're discovered."

"Done," said Ice. "You're playing them on Monday."

Grease drove us fifty kilometres north of Brunswick Valley into a desolate area interspersed with scrubby fields. Bethel Station Regional was on an empty stretch of road with no nearby communities.

I thought we'd be safe playing so far away from home, but the first person I saw was Floyd Wheeler, who used to go to St. Croix.

"What's *he* doing here?" I muttered to Julie.

"His parents split up," she explained. "His mom lives here, but his dad's still in St. Croix."

I groaned. "He'll tell all his friends in St. Croix about us."

"Grease will keep him quiet," Ice offered. "He's good at that. Just say the word."

"No, thank you," I said quickly. "We'll take our chances. Let's call the St. Croix coach back and arrange the game sooner — before word gets around."

As soon as we took the field, Floyd Wheeler trotted over, a smirk on his face.

"Haven't I seen you somewhere before?" he said sarcastically.

No answer.

"I thought you guys played for Brunswick Valley," Floyd persisted.

I still didn't answer.

He looked around at the rest of our team. "You *are* Brunswick Valley. You dropped out of the league. What's going on?"

"Same team, different name," I said. "So what?"

"So does the league know you're the same team?" Floyd threatened. "You haven't played my old school yet, have you? I'll be in St. Croix this weekend. They'll be interested to hear that 'Cemetery Road' is actually Brunswick Valley."

We knew Floyd from past games. He was a rough, tough defender who liked to intimidate his opponents. He was bigger than any of us — older, too. He had repeated a grade along the way and was old enough to be in high school. Brandon in particular had been on the receiving end of Floyd's attentions in earlier games, and was already eyeing him nervously as we took our positions to start.

Floyd pointed at Magic and instructed two of his defenders, "Stay with him all the time. Even when he's nowhere near the ball, stay on him." He looked at Brandon. "I'll take care of my little friend here."

Ten minutes into the game Floyd crashed into Brandon from behind, sending him sprawling on his face.

He leaned over as if to pull Brandon to his feet. I could see Floyd's fingers turn white with the force of his grip on Brandon's arm.

Ice made his way onto the pitch. He motioned for Grease, too. Grease was wearing his usual camouflage pants and boots and yellow muscle shirt, and he'd just had his strip of hair coloured purple instead of green.

The Bethel Station coach called, "Wait. What … Who's this?"

"He's our trainer," said Ice. "Don't forget your first aid kit, Mr. Trainer."

Grease returned to the van, brought out a black box and knelt beside Brandon. He reached into his first aid kit — it was plastic with "Mastercraft" written on the side — and produced a wrench. Brandon sat up.

Grease tapped Brandon's knees with the wrench, looked up at Ice and the referee, and gave a thumbs up.

"He says there's nothing broken," said Ice.

As Ice and Grease left the field, they passed close to Floyd.

Ice said, "Grease takes it very personally when one of his friends gets hurt. If he thought someone had set out to hurt one of his friends, he'd probably like a word with that person after the game. Wouldn't you, Grease?"

Grease looked hard at Floyd and nodded slowly.

After that Floyd seemed reluctant to tackle Brandon, and he soon headed home across from Jillian.

Bethel Station pressed hard for an equalizer, and Brian had to make some good saves, but we were still a goal up at halftime.

"We need another goal to feel safe," I warned during the break.

"We're not making much headway against their defence," Magic admitted.

"Do the Syncopation Surprise move — the one we practiced," Ice suggested. "I'll give you the signal when to do it, like this." He sliced his arm backwards and forwards in a Z shape. "Shay, you and Julie start it."

This was a move we'd practiced at the Cemetery Road in the sunny spotlight one evening when Ice showed up to watch. He'd explained that the move was a good one to use to split a solid defence. "I call it the zig-zag-zap move, but its real name is the Syncopation Surprise."

I'd looked at him doubtfully and said, "Synco-what?"

"Syncopation," he'd said. "It's from music. It's when you upset an anticipated rhythm. In soccer, it means you set up a rhythm of passing — a pattern — then you deliberately break it, and catch the defenders on the hop. They'll follow the pattern of passing you've started. They can't help it. It's instinct, like when you get in the groove of a piece of music."

"How do you know these moves?" I'd asked.

He'd shrugged. "It's just stuff I've picked up."

Halfway through the second half, Toby cleared the ball from our goalmouth to me. As I trapped it under my foot, I saw Ice give the signal.

I said, "Julie — now!"

Julie raced toward the wing. I led her with a pass and she swept the ball back across the field to the opposite wing, where Jessica was waiting. She took the ball forwards a little ways and passed back across the field to Jillian. The defenders, as Ice had predicted, followed the direction of the ball, moving one way and then the other with the pattern of our passes. Now they turned to the other wing, where Brandon waited, as if for the next pass. But instead of sending the ball back across the field, Jillian pushed it along the touchline to where Magic waited, left unguarded for the first time in the game. He trotted into the penalty area, took the ball around the goalkeeper and tapped it into the net.

The game ended with the score at 2–0. We were winners again.

11 Lies

I hated lying to Grandad, but didn't know what else to do.

I'd decided we should have a team meeting before we played St. Croix. We were two points behind them and this was the final game for both teams.

On my way out, I peeked into the living room. Grandad was in the armchair, his eyes closed. I turned to tiptoe out.

"Are you off to play soccer again?" he said suddenly.

"I thought you were asleep. I won't be long. Will you be okay?"

"Of course I'll be okay. Julie's mom will be over later. Are you playing at the Back Field again?"

"Er ... yes."

"Is it a school game?"

"Just a kick around with Julie, Toby and the others."

"When's the next school game?"

"I'm … not sure," I stammered.

"Be sure to let me know. It seems like a long time since you've played a school game at home and I've been able to watch you. I miss seeing you play, and seeing Miss Little coach, too."

Grandad and Miss Little always talked soccer when they met at parents' evenings and other school events.

"Miss Little's a good coach," Grandad went on, leaning back in his chair. "She's firm but fair, the way a coach should be. You know, I never could stand rules when I was growing up. That's why I was always in trouble — until I played soccer. The Newcastle Wanderers' coach laid down the rules with an iron hand! We grumbled about it, but looking back, it was the best thing for me."

He sat up, and looked steadily at me. "Now you know where your dad got his instinct for breaking the rules, don't you? He got it from me. Only difference — soccer saved me, and your dad never got into soccer — more's the pity." Grandad sighed and looked away from me, then his voice lightened. "Go on, have a good time," he said.

Julie was adjusting her shoe at the end of her driveway.

She greeted me with, "Where did you tell your grandad we were going?"

"The Back Field."

"Good. That's what I told Mom."

"What's wrong with saying we're going to the Cemetery Road?" I suggested.

"Nothing … except they would want to know why we weren't playing at the Back Field, and then what would we tell them?"

"We'd have to lie — again. It's funny how once you start lying, you have to keep on lying."

We were first at the Cemetery Road. It had started to rain, so we climbed the bank and sheltered under the trees until the others arrived. I was about to start the meeting when a familiar deep, raspy voice interrupted.

"Why don't you just go down to the river and jump in if you want to get soaking wet? It'd be a lot quicker."

"We're having a team meeting," I told Ice.

"I thought you were having a picnic."

"We can't meet at our homes or at school," I explained.

"Why don't you use my house? Grease is waiting with the van."

"How come he's here too?"

"I asked him to be on standby."

"We don't have money for gas."

"He won't mind."

We found Grease and the van at the Portage Street gate. He emerged from under the hood and pointed to Brandon's leg, raising his eyebrows. Brandon held out his hand and wobbled it. Grease gave a thumbs up and grunted.

"They're having quite a conversation," said Ice.

As we climbed in, I asked, "Where do you live, anyway?"

"Snob Hill," he said.

"You're kidding."

Snob Hill was really Woodland Crescent. The houses there were big and secluded and had huge grounds. It was on the edge of town on the side of a hill. Grease drove us up and turned into a long tree-lined driveway. We stopped in front of a low, white house that looked as if it should be on a ranch in Mexico.

Silently, we followed Ice and Grease inside. Over the intercom in the entrance hall, Ice called, "Mrs. P., I've brought some friends over."

"Who's Mrs. P.?" I whispered.

"Mrs. Pettipas — our housekeeper."

"Where are your parents?" I wondered.

"My mother's in Alberta somewhere, I think — I haven't seen her for years — and my father's away. He's away a lot."

"On business?"

Ice hesitated. "Sort of."

He led us into a wood-panelled room and we all sat around a long table in chunky wooden chairs with leather armrests.

A woman, smartly dressed in what looked like a

gray business suit, entered behind us, and said, "Good evening, Mr. Jeremy. Would your guests like some refreshments?"

I looked at Ice and mouthed, "Mr. Jeremy?"

"That's my real name," Ice muttered. "Mrs. P.'s the only one who uses it." He answered Mrs. Pettipas, "They'll have lemonade and cookies, please."

"What would you and Mr. Grease like?"

"Grease and I will have our usual evening beverage, please."

"Does Grease live here, too?" I asked, as Mrs. Pettipas left the room.

Grease was sitting in a big leather chair at the end of the room with his boots on the table.

"Sometimes."

Mrs. Pettipas returned with our refreshments. Then she handed Ice and Grease each a glass of red wine.

Ice rapped on the table. "Okay, Shay — bring this team meeting to order."

We stared at the wine in amazement.

He looked at me. "Go on. You're the boss."

"We have to make sure we don't give up an early goal against St. Croix, because if they get ahead you know how tough their defence is," I said. "So we'll play four at the back and four in the middle, with two strikers."

Grease leaned forward, slapped Brandon on the shoulder, and nodded. Everyone except Ice and Grease was sitting forward attentively. I felt like the president of a company.

"Okay — you know we're going to be recognized by St. Croix right away. They'd like nothing more than to *finish* our team. If we get to play — let's go out with a win."

I looked at Ice. "Do you want to say anything?"

"I've got an idea," Ice said thoughtfully. "This strategy is called the Third Force Strike."

Julie looked at Ice, shaking her head.

"What?" he said. "You think I'm full of it, darling, don't you?"

"Don't call me darling."

Ice ignored her complaint and went on, "It means when you have two opposing forces at stalemate, you can work a breakthrough by introducing an unexpected new power — a third force. It's a term that's used in psychology and power games." He'd been leaning back in the chair beside me at the head of the table, sipping his wine elegantly. Now he suddenly sat forward. "In soccer it means you set up your main strike force — that's you, Magic and Brandon — and then you sneak in a third striker who drifts in from somewhere unexpected."

I said, "How do you know this stuff?"

"Never mind," said Ice. "Who's the least likely striker here?"

We looked around the table at one another.

"Suppose you were playing against the Wanderers," Ice pressed. "Which of you would you least expect to score a goal?"

Linh-Mai said quietly and apologetically, "I guess that'd be me."

"Then you'll be our Third Force, darling," said Ice. "This is how we'll do it …"

When Ice had finished explaining how we'd carry out the move, and while we passed the cookies around the table one last time, I asked Ice where the washroom was. He said down the hallway on the left.

The washroom was like something out of a magazine, with big, old fashioned taps, and scented soap, and thick fluffy hand towels hanging on the back of the door. On the way out I noticed, through the open door of the room across the hallway, a set of photographs on the wall. The figures in the photographs looked like soccer players. I crossed the hall and took a step inside the room. I knew I was being nosy, but I was so intrigued by the photographs I couldn't help it.

The room was like a small study, with a desk in the centre and behind it a wall lined with book shelves. The photographs hung on the wall beside me. They were all of the same person, a young soccer player. In one picture he stood with his foot on a soccer ball, his arms folded, grinning. His soccer shirt bore the words "Montreal Marvels." In another he stood among some suited adults, holding a trophy. A caption beneath read "Young Soccer Player of the Year." There were more pictures — of a team, and of the young soccer player in action. I looked more closely. I tried adding a few years to the face, and a few inches and pounds to the body, and imagined a black sweatshirt and black pants and a long black trench coat instead of the soccer uniform.

It was Ice.

Suddenly, I heard footsteps and Mrs. Pettipas appeared in the door.

"That's young Mr. Jeremy, when we lived in Montreal. He was quite the soccer star in those days." She looked fondly at the photographs, then whispered, "He doesn't like people to see these."

As I turned to follow Mrs. Pettipas from the room, I noticed another set of photographs. These were shots of a man in a New York Kickers uniform.

I didn't mention the photographs to anyone else. If Ice wanted them kept a secret, I wasn't going to betray him.

When I got home, a news program was introducing a story about the American Soccer League.

"Dan Field, of the New York Kickers, has once again been named American Soccer League player of the year. He is the highest scoring player, and also the highest paid player, in the league."

"We never made big money when we were playing," Grandad muttered.

I looked with interest. The soccer player on TV was the man in the photographs at Ice's house.

Why would a photo of Dan Field be hanging in Ice's house?

I thought of the pictures I had in my room. I had posters of Iain Hume and Paul Stalteri, the Canadian midfielders, and I had photos of Grandad: one of him looking young in his Newcastle Wanderers uniform, and another of him in the flower shop surrounded by bouquets. I also had an old photo of my parents that Grandad said was taken on their wedding day. Suddenly, I had a crazy thought that Dan Field could be a relative. It would explain Ice's interest in the sport.

Surely, Dan Field couldn't be Ice's …

No. It didn't make sense. If you had a famous father, you wouldn't keep something like that a secret.

"How long will you continue to play in the States while your family remains up in Canada?" the interviewer asked Field.

"I won't discuss my family," Field said tersely.

"How do you feel about being named Player of the Year?" the interviewer tried.

"Proud, of course," said Dan Field.

The interviewer pressed on. "You're the highest paid player in the history of the ASL. What kind of pressure is there to produce at the level you have been for the past few years?"

Dan Field looked at the interviewer as if he was a

stick of rhubarb. "What do you think?" he said, and walked away.

"He's a friendly fellow, isn't he?" commented Grandad as the interviewer closed.

"Did you ever hear of a team called the Montreal Marvels?" I asked Grandad incidentally.

"They were the best young players in the country," he replied. "They played all over Canada, the United States and South America — as a training team for the Canadian Soccer League. Lots of the players went on to play professionally."

★ ★ ★

Michelle, James and Josh were deep in conversation when Julie and I entered the classroom on the day of the St. Croix game.

"It's true. My dad heard it at work. The soccer team's going to get kicked out of the league!" exclaimed Michelle.

I joined the group and said casually, "Who's getting kicked out of what?"

Michelle repeated, "A team from Brunswick Valley is getting kicked out of the league because no one knows who the players are or where they come from. It's like a ghost team. And that's not all. They say it'd be too bad if they get kicked out, because they rule."

Brian had joined us. "Did they say anything about the goalkeeper?"

Before Michelle could reply, Brian gasped.

"Sorry, Brian. I think I stepped on your toe," Julie said. She turned to Michelle and went on quickly, "I like how you've got your hair today."

"I had it done at Dar's Cuts 'N Styles last night," said Michelle, patting her hair.

James and Josh drifted away.

Miss Little was in the cafeteria at lunch time. She leaned down beside me and whispered, "I went to see Ms. Dugalici last night."

"What did she say?" I asked hopefully.

"She listened."

"Then I bumped into a teacher who mentioned a phantom team from Brunswick Valley whom St. Croix had to beat today in order to win the league championship. She said the result didn't really matter because the team was going to get suspended on the grounds that it didn't represent a real school."

"Hmm. Lots of strange rumours going around," I said.

"I know," said Miss Little. "I just thought I'd mention it, in case the phantom team needed any support."

Ice came to the fence at noon recess.

Grease was leaning against the van in the school parking lot. Brandon wandered over to him.

"Charlie Finch, from the league, called me this morning," Ice announced.

"Were you in French class again?"

"In gym class," Ice corrected me. "It was noisy, so it didn't matter. Now listen. I think we may have problems in the game this afternoon. Charlie told me he'd had a call from the St. Croix coach saying he had concerns about the legitimacy of the Wanderers. He started to ask me exactly where Cemetery Road School was."

"What did you say?"

"I said he'd have to excuse me because I was teaching — he thinks I'm on the staff at Cemetery Road School, remember — and I'd call him back as soon as possible. He called me twice more after that — I saw his name on call display — so I got one of the girls in my class to answer and pretend she was the school secretary."

"What did she tell him?"

"That Mr. Field was still in class and then had a meeting."

"Mr. Field?" I said. "Who's he?"

"Field — that's my name," said Ice.

Julie started, "So you're called Ice to make a joke with your name — Ice Field — and not because you're ..."

"Not because I'm so cool I'm ice — right?"

"Right."

"That's right," said Ice. "Although I am."

"What?"

"Cool as ice."

Julie shook her head.

Ice concluded, "Anyway just thought I'd warn you Charlie Finch is on the trail." He slapped me on the shoulder. "Stay cool. I'll see you at the Cemetery Road before the game."

Julie and I walked across to the van with him. Grease and Brandon were looking at the engine. Grease closed the hood.

"Ready, Grease?" said Ice.

Grease grunted.

Brandon looked at Grease.

"Hi, Brandon," said Ice. "Are you ready for the big game? We'll need some goals from you."

"He's worried about the way St. Croix plays," I said.

Brandon had confided to me earlier that he couldn't get Floyd's brutal tackle in the game against Bethel Station out of his mind, and he was afraid the St. Croix defenders would be like Floyd, and set out to hurt him.

"Their defenders like to intimidate the other team's strikers," I explained.

"Is that right?" said Ice. "Don't worry, Brandon. Grease will be there. He'll keep an eye out for you."

Grease grunted again.

"Let's go," said Ice. "See you later, boys and girls."

Brandon looked at Grease, his lips working furiously, making little popping sounds. "B— ... B— ... Bye, G ... Grease," he said at last.

Grease turned back to face Brandon and a hissing sound started from his lips. "S-s-s-s ... See you, Brandon."

Ice, who'd been looking from one to the other, smiled. "It's not just about the soccer, is it?" he said quietly.

It wasn't until Ice and Grease had left, and I was reflecting that it was strange how everyone seemed to know Ice as just Ice, when the name "Field" zapped me like a jolt of static electricity. So Dan Field was Ice's father. That explained how Ice knew so much about soccer. Not only had he played at a high level himself, but on top of that — his dad was a major star. But why keep his own soccer talent a secret? I thought of the photographs I'd seen of Ice, the proud young soccer player, enjoying his days of glory before, for some reason, he'd turned his back on them.

What had happened to turn that emerging soccer star into the shady, black clad, slouching Ice we knew?

12 Coach Ice

As soon as classes ended, Julie and I ran back to Riverside Drive. We couldn't take our soccer gear to school, so we had to rush home to change, tell our folks we had a pick-up game, and hurry back to meet at the Cemetery Road.

Grandad was in the flower shop. There were no customers and he was sitting behind the counter reading a book of poetry.

He looked up and said, "I've found a poem I haven't seen for years. It was one of my favourites when I was a youngster your age. It's an old rebel song. They say the Iceni — the ancient tribe of Britons — sung it before their last battle, when they knew their rebellion against the Romans was doomed. Do you want to hear it?"

I nodded.

Grandad recited, looking at me and not at the book, "Between the mud and the sun, there are battles we've won. Ere shade ends our story, let's fashion brief glory." He added, "I learned that when I was a kid, and I've never forgotten it."

I said, "I like the bit about 'brief glory.'"

"Maybe that's the best we can hope for — a bit of brief glory," said Grandad. He sounded sad.

"I'm off to play soccer with Julie and the others down at the Back Field," I lied.

"Have fun," Grandad said, and went back to his poems.

I hurried next door, where Julie, in her soccer kit, was pacing backwards and forwards across her driveway, Little Sis in tow.

"I can't leave until Mom gets home from work," she said.

While I waited with her, I recited Grandad's poem, which had stuck in my memory.

Julie repeated the last line and wondered, "Is that what we're trying to do — get some brief glory?"

Little Sis whined and Julie said, "There's no sign of Mom. You'd better go on. I'll catch up with you."

At the cemetery I wandered up the bank and sat under the trees while I waited for the others to arrive. The sun was so low now that even with the dwindling foliage, it hardly shone on the Cemetery Road.

With the Wanderers facing discovery, and trouble, I wondered whether it would be better if the team had never existed. But everything we'd done together with

Ice behind us, playing better than ever — they were like those moments of brief glory, like in Grandad's poem. The memories crowded into my mind, and seemed to make everything worthwhile, whatever the cost. I thought of plodding Toby, planting himself in front of goal like a big, solid shield … of Flyin' Brian, clutching the ball after flinging himself across the goal to make an acrobatic save … of Magic, his arm raised in triumph after a dazzling goal … of Julie, racing down the soccer field, her hair streaming behind her … of Brandon, talking …

For an instant, a sliver of sun glinted on the old road beneath me. Then the glorious, golden spotlight was gone.

Julie scrambled up the bank and joined me.

"We've lost our spotlight," I said, nodding at the shady road below us.

"We're going to lose the Wanderers, too," said Julie. "And we're going to be in big trouble."

She gave me her hand and pulled me to my feet.

"Was it all worth it?" I asked.

She brushed the back of my hand briefly with her fingertips. "Oh yes."

The twins and Linh-Mai appeared below us on the Cemetery Road.

Jillian greeted us with, "We're found out. Mom saw Mrs. Stuart in the Food Mart and told her it was nice we could play soccer on the Back Field in the evenings. That's where we tell her we're playing when we're at Wanderers' games. Mrs. Stuart said that was strange because we were suspended and weren't allowed on the Back Field."

Jessica took over. "Mom got the whole story out of us and she's mad and says she's going to have a chat with us when she gets home from work tonight about rules and lying. She called Mrs. Stuart and she said she was going to see Mr. Justason after school. So he's finding out — right now."

"We're going to be found out anyway," I said. "Let's hope we can get the game in before Mr. Justason and Mrs. Stuart can do anything to stop it."

Brian raced down to the Cemetery Road shouting, "Are we going to play like superstars or what?" By the time the rest of the team had arrived, he was alternately running from side to side in furious bursts of speed, and jumping for imaginary shots on his goal, urging, "Let's go, folks!"

Linh-Mai's fists were clenched as she muttered, "Third force … drift in …"

Toby teased gently, "You're a killer, Linh-Mai," and the twins giggled nervously.

Magic and Brandon fired a soccer ball between them.

Toby said, "Ready, cap?"

They all stopped and looked at me.

I nodded.

They followed me silently to the Portage Street gate, where Ice and Grease waited with the van. The only one who spoke as we climbed in was Brandon, who said a quiet "H— ... Hi," to Grease.

Grease bobbed his head to one side in acknowledgement.

We stayed silent on the way to St. Croix until Linh-Mai said she had to go to the bathroom. Grease stopped by the highway and she ran in the woods.

"Sorry, everyone," she mumbled as she climbed back in the van. "I'm so nervous."

Ice, holding the door open and helping her into the van, said, "You'll be all right, darling."

As we drove through the commercial strip on the outskirts of St. Croix, Ice turned to us from the passenger seat and said, "In case I don't get to say this in the heat of the game, I want you to know — it's been a blast, boys and girls. Whatever happens now — let's go out in a blaze of glory!"

On Main Street, just before he turned into the road to St. Croix Middle School, Grease opened the window and shouted, "Glory!"

Brandon echoed, "G — ... Glory!"

We all shouted, "Glory!"

★ ★ ★

St. Croix Middle School is like Brunswick Valley School — old and made of brick. But it's much bigger. It's a box stuck between a slab of black, the parking lot, and a patch of green, the playing field.

Before we even climbed from the van, a man, dapper in his green blazer and white shirt, hurried towards us.

"Is that the St. Croix coach?" muttered Ice.

"No way," I said. "Mr. Pellerin has a track suit in the St. Croix colours."

"Then that'll be my friend Charlie Finch," said Ice.

Mr. Finch had straight, square shoulders and a square chin with a dimple. His thin, sandy hair flopped over one side of his forehead.

Ice jumped from the van and held out his hand. "Mr. Finch — Charlie."

Mr. Finch hesitated a moment before shaking Ice's hand. "Are you — er — Ice? Mr. Ice?"

"Just Ice, please," said Ice.

"Ice ... I imagined someone a little ... older. You're very young to be a teacher."

"I'm a student teacher," said Ice.

"I've been trying to get in touch with you."

"I know. I apologize for not getting back to you. I've been so busy ..."

"I called but there was no answer at the school."

"Our secretary has been away sick, and I've had so

many meetings, not to mention teaching my regular classes."

"I need to know more about Cemetery Road School," Mr. Finch said cautiously. "Where exactly do you play soccer?"

"The Church allows us to use a part of their grounds, and … If you'd excuse me for a moment …" Ice turned to us. "Get yourselves ready, boys and girls. Hurry down to the field and warm up." He turned back to Mr. Finch. "Cemetery Road School is a small private institution, new and not yet very well known. The principal asked me to tell you he's sorry he can't be here, and to thank you for all your work for the league." Ice walked towards the soccer field, saying, "How long have you been president?"

Mr. Finch set off with Ice, saying, "I've had the job for two years …"

"It must be *very* demanding …" I heard Ice say before they were out of earshot.

Toby, watching them, shook his head and said admiringly, "Ice should be a con man."

"He is a con man — fortunately for us," I said. "You heard him, everybody. Let's go."

We jogged around the school, past Ice and Mr. Finch, to the field.

Mr. Pellerin, the St. Croix coach, held out his arms as we rounded the school. "Wait just a moment."

I said, "You'll have to talk to our coach," and led

the Wanderers past him and onto the field. The St. Croix players were already warming up at one end, and the referee was looking at his watch.

"How soon can you be ready to play?" he asked.

"As soon as you like," I said, thinking the sooner the better, before we're discovered.

"Then we'll start the coaches' competition in a couple of minutes, and the game will follow immediately after that," said the referee. He joined Coach Pellerin on the sideline.

I'd forgotten about the coaches' competition. Every year before the start of the last league game all the coaches were invited to compete in a series of drills. I'd never taken much notice of it, because Miss Little had never taken part.

Ice and Mr. Finch appeared around the corner of the school, walking slowly and deep in conversation. Mr. Finch had his hand on Ice's shoulder. A short, white haired man was with them.

Coach Pellerin and the referee, who'd been talking and laughing together, hurried across.

A few minutes later Mr. Finch called, "Would the captains join us, please?"

I trotted over to the little group at the same time as Doozie Dougan ran across from the St. Croix team.

"We're going to give you losers a whipping — if you get to play," Doozie threatened quietly.

Mr. Finch started, "Serious allegations about the

authenticity of the Cemetery Road Wanderers and their eligibility to compete in the league have been made."

"The team is not just ineligible," the St. Croix coach interrupted. "It's a fraud. Cemetery Road School doesn't even exist. These players" — he waved his arm in the direction of the Wanderers — "are the Brunswick Valley School team, which resigned from the league weeks ago."

"I know Brunswick Valley resigned," agreed Mr. Finch. "But I have only your claim that Cemetery Road School does not exist, while this gentleman" — he indicated Ice — "tells me he is a student teacher at Cemetery Road and is coach of the soccer team."

"He's not a student teacher, and he's certainly not a coach," snapped Mr. Pellerin.

Mr. Finch went on, "I intend to call the Department of Education now to verify the authenticity of the school, and then I'll make a ruling. Meanwhile, teams, coaches and spectators are here, so while I make my call, let's go ahead with the coaches competition, then let the kids play. That way it won't be an entirely wasted evening. Mr. Leavitt, the league vice president" — he nodded to his companion — "will conduct the coaches' competition."

Mr. Leavitt announced through a megaphone, "Would the coaches come forward, please?"

The coaches stood beside the field. Coach Pellerin,

shaking his head, joined them.

"May I first introduce the St. Croix Middle School coach, Mr. Ross Pellerin," Mr. Leavitt boomed.

Coach Pellerin had played for one of the Canadian Soccer League teams before he came to St. Croix to teach. He had short fair hair and a sort of stubbly beard, like film stars have. He strutted onto the field, his arms raised, fists clenched, to a huge cheer from the spectators and his team.

The Bethel Station, Keswick Narrows and Westfield Ridge coaches followed as Mr. Leavitt introduced them to polite, lukewarm applause from the crowd.

Mr. Leavitt announced, "I believe Cemetery Road School will not offer a participant." He looked towards where we clustered around Ice. I had to admit he looked an unlikely candidate, slouched on the sideline in his long trench coat and sombre black outfit, with his long, unruly hair hanging in front of his face.

Brian and Linh-Mai looked hopefully, briefly, at him.

Ice held up his hand, shook his head and laughed. "No way."

"As I thought," Mr. Leavitt went on through his megaphone, "Cemetery Road will not offer a participant."

A few jeers arose from the St. Croix students and spectators, and I noticed smirks on the faces of the home players.

Linh-Mai's head drooped.

Brian kicked at the ground.

Ice muttered, "Sorry, guys."

I tugged at his sleeve. "It doesn't matter."

Ice said suddenly, "Oh — what the heck." He shouted to the announcer, "Wait!"

I said quietly, "I don't know why you feel the way you do about soccer, and whether it's something to do with your dad" — Ice looked sharply at me — "but — you don't have to do this. Don't go out there just for us."

Mr. Leavitt said, "Perhaps we do have a participant from Cemetery Road after all ..."

"I'm not going out there just for you guys. It's for me, too."

He tore off his trench coat to reveal a track suit in the Wanderers' colours.

"I'll need a pair of cleats," he said.

Toby offered, "I've got the biggest feet. Try mine." He quickly unlaced his cleats.

Ice sat to put them on. He rose and took a few steps forward, pushing his wild hair back from his eyes.

Linh-Mai said timidly, "Here."

She plucked her hair band from her head. Ice bent down and Linh-Mai tucked the band behind his ears, pulling his hair back from his forehead and out of his eyes.

"Thanks, darling," said Ice.

"Cool," Brandon said.

"Go, man," Grease called.

"Y— ... Yeah!" Brandon yelled.

Ice trotted on to the pitch. He was greeted by silence.

I clapped and shouted, "Go, Coach Ice!"

Ice turned, raised his hands, and clapped in our direction.

Suddenly, he was no longer the black clad, slouching misfit he seemed so bent on presenting himself to be. Suddenly — he was a soccer star.

The Wanderers cheered.

"The first round will be the dribbling contest," Mr. Leavitt announced.

Each coach stood behind a row of pylons with a soccer ball at his feet.

"The first to dribble the ball through the pylons is the winner," Mr. Leavitt intoned. "Ready — go!"

Ice and Coach Pellerin were level all the way. Mr. Pellerin drew ahead near the finishing line, but slipped and fell. His ball rolled into the path of Ice, who gathered it with his left foot, while his right foot kept control of his own. While Coach Pellerin picked himself up, Ice took both balls round his last pylon before passing one back. The St. Croix coach crossed the finishing line just ahead.

"Where did Ice learn to dribble like that?" muttered Brian.

Mr. Leavitt boomed, "Coach Pellerin wins!"

Wild applause erupted from the spectators and the St. Croix team.

"The next event is the ball control contest, in which the coach who keeps his soccer ball in the air longest, without using his hands, wins," said Mr. Leavitt.

All the coaches quickly lost control, except Ice, who looked as if he was in another world as he juggled the ball with his head, feet, and knees.

Next the coaches had to kick from one side of the field to the other and land the ball in a hoop. Only Mr. Pellerin and Coach Ice succeeded.

"The St. Croix coach and the Cemetery Road Wanderers coach are tied for first place with one round left," Mr. Leavitt announced. "The final event is the penalty shootout. The coaches will take penalty kicks in turn, dropping out if they fail to score. We have a special guest goalkeeper for this event — please welcome ... Jordan Thorne of the Eastern Canadian Cougars!"

Brian gasped, "He's the best goalkeeper in the league."

Jordan Thorne was like a gangly giant — tall and broad shouldered, with long arms and huge hands. He grinned shyly and gave a little wave in response to the applause.

The coaches lined up to take their penalty shots.

When it was Coach Pellerin's turn, he called loudly, "Hi, Jordan."

The goalkeeper nodded. "Nice to see you, Ross."

Coach Pellerin shot and scored.

Ice stepped forward.

Jordan Thorne said uncertainly, "Ice? Ice Field?"

Ice nodded, then coolly scored.

The Bethel Station coach was knocked out when he missed the goal, and in the next round Jordan Thorne stopped the Westfield Ridge coach's shot.

Coach Pellerin fired the ball past the goalkeeper and said to Ice, "Think you can do another lucky shot?"

Ice kicked left, past Jordan Thorne, who'd dived right.

The St. Croix coach took a long run up and blasted the ball. Jordan Thorne tipped it wide of the post. A groan went up from the spectators.

"If the Cemetery Road coach can score — he wins the coaches' competition," Mr. Leavitt announced.

Ice took his time placing the ball. He took three steps back and looked up at Jordan Thorne. With his eyes still on the goalkeeper, Ice trotted forwards. Jordan Thorne dived right. Ice shot left. The ball rocketed into the net.

Jordan Thorne picked himself up, shook Ice's hand, and said, "Same old tricks."

Ice said, "Good goalkeeping, old buddy."

"I wish you were still with us," said Jordan Thorne.

"I declare the Cemetery Road coach the winner!" Mr. Leavitt boomed.

A few of the spectators applauded politely while the Wanderers cheered.

As Ice returned to us, I said, "You were with the *Cougars?*"

Linh-Mai looked at Ice with shining eyes.

"How did you know to kick left?" said Brian.

"I've played with Jordan lots of times," said Ice. "He always looks in the direction he's going to dive."

"When ... How ..." Brian started.

Ice went on quickly, "Let's get ready for the game."

As we prepared to take the field, the St. Croix coach sauntered over. "Look, fellas," he said. "When Mr. Finch discovers Cemetery Road School doesn't exist, there's going to be trouble. But if you concede the game, I'll drop the accusations, and that'll be the end of it."

Ice looked at me.

I shook my head.

"We can play the game," Coach Pellerin pressed. "All you have to do is tell your team to throw it."

Ice looked at me again. "You're captain. What do you say?"

"I say — glory."

"Meaning — ?" the St. Croix coach demanded.

"Meaning you can shove your offer," said Ice.

Coach Pellerin's eyes narrowed. "You'll regret this. We'll beat you — then we'll destroy you."

13 Glory

Mostly, when I think of the game, I remember the silence at the end, broken only by the applause of a lone Wanderers supporter.

The play comes back to me in a series of high-lights, with me doing the commentary as if I'm on the sports channel in the round up of the soccer games, with the score appearing at the bottom of the screen after every goal.

When I reach the final clip, it's as if the sound is turned off.

The referee blows the whistle to start and a long pass from St. Croix's Tiny Jones sends John Hawler on his way toward the Wanderers' goal. Linh-Mai bars his way forward but he pushes her to the ground. Toby robs Hawler of the ball but their legs tangle and they fall. The referee runs into the goalmouth. The players are waiting for him to whistle. Meanwhile the ball trickles clear of Toby and Hawler, and St. Croix's Holt taps it into the net while the Wanderers' goalkeeper is distracted by the referee beside him. Now the whistle sounds and it's … it's … it's not for Hawler's foul on Linh-Mai, but for a goal. St. Croix has scored. And it's not just a goal, but also a yellow card — a caution — for Toby, for his tackle on Hawler. Quan is warning Hawler for the way he tackled Linh-Mai. And … I don't know what he said, but the referee has produced a red card which means Quan is off! The visitors are down to ten players in only the fifth minute of the game.

St. Croix Middle School 1 — Cemetery Road Wanderers 0

Brandon dribbles the ball across the goalmouth as Magic runs in a scissor movement. Brandon backheels the ball for Magic to collect and fire into the goal.

St. Croix Middle School 1 — Cemetery Road Wanderers 1

Dougan crashes heavily into Brandon from behind, knocking him to the ground. The Wanderers' assistant coach — the gentleman in the camouflage pants and yellow muscle shirt — is being restrained by the Wanderers' coach from running onto the field to confront Hawler about his dangerous tackle.

… Now Dougan is through the Wanderers' defence but Flyin' Brian dives to smother the ball. Dougan kicks it from his hands and prods it into the net.

The St. Croix coach pumps his fists in celebration, while the Wanderers' coach shouts something at the referee, who looks in his direction and ... raises the yellow card. Now the Wanderers' coach will have to mind his behaviour or he'll be banned from the touchline.

St. Croix Middle School 2 – Cemetery Road Wanderers 1

Halfway through the second half the teams are at a stalemate. There's a disturbance at the side of the field. Three people, a tall gentleman and two ladies, one of them short and wearing a business suit, the other big and wearing a long, plain dress, are arguing with the league president. They seem — at least two of them seem — to be demanding that the Wanderers leave the field, but Mr. Finch is insisting the game continue.

Back to the play, where Hawler is running at the Wanderers' goal, pursued by Linh-Mai, who's half his size. She overtakes him ... turns and prepares to tackle ... Hawler closes in on her, towering above her, and ... falls over. Linh-Mai didn't tackle Hawler, but he's on the ground, holding his leg in agony, and the referee has given a penalty! This time it's the Wanderers' assistant coach restraining the coach, who is shouting something at the referee ... calling him a ... I can't believe what he called him. I've never heard a referee called that before. I've never heard anyone called that before. The referee looks shocked — so do some of the adult specta-

tors — and it's a red card for the Wanderers' coach. He'll have to spend the rest of the game well clear of the touchline. Hawler, who seems to have made a quick recovery, prepares to take the penalty. He shoots high to the right. Flyin' Brian launches himself across the goal and his finger tips, clawing desperately, turn the ball against the post. As he lands heavily, Hawler, following up, taps the ball into the net.

St. Croix Middle School 3 – Cemetery Road Wanderers 1

Shay, Julie, and Magic move up the field, passing and overlapping one another as the opposing defenders challenge them. Jones smacks into Magic, leaving him sprawled on the ground. Julie loses her footing and falls as she is shouldercharged by another defender. Shay keeps running. He rounds one defender, spins away from another, and, seeing the goalkeeper on the edge of his penalty box, chips the ball over him and into the net.

The crowd is silent.

St. Croix Middle School 3 – Cemetery Road Wanderers 2

The Wanderers are pressing for an equalizer. The St. Croix goalkeeper rolls the ball out to Tiny Jones, who shapes to pass left but finds Jillian in the way. He prepares to pass right, but Flip is there. He starts forward, but seeing Julie ahead, passes back to his goalkeeper. Julie speeds past him in a whirling mass of flying hair and pumping elbows. The goalkeeper dives for the ball, but the Wanderers' midfielder is too fast and pushes it under him into the net.

Not a sound from the spectators.

Wait — yes, there is.

One spectator, standing alone far back from the field, who arrived just in time to see the Wanderers score, is applauding. She's a tall, blonde lady, with big, round glasses ...

St. Croix Middle School 3 – Cemetery Road Wanderers 3

With only seconds left and the teams still tied, the Wanderers keep pressing. The St. Croix goalkeeper clears from the melee of defenders and forwards jostling in his goalmouth. Shay traps it, looks quickly around ... Gives some kind of signal ... The St. Croix defenders swarm around the Wanderers ... There's no room for anyone to move and no chance to score. But wait ... Linh-Mai, running from deep behind the attack, is drifting toward the St. Croix goal, unnoticed by the home defenders. Shay twists clear of two defenders and passes to her. Suddenly aware of the danger, Hawler turns on Linh-Mai with a roar. She pokes the ball past him, and past the goalkeeper. She reels back as Hawler thunders towards her. At the last moment Toby throws himself between them. Hawler bounces off him. The whistle sounds as the ball trickles into the goal.

The referee points to Toby; it's obstruction. No goal.

Mr. Finch strides onto the field. "Goal — and end of game!"

The St. Croix supporters watch in dejected silence.

The solitary Wanderers supporter, the tall blonde lady with the big round glasses, applauds and slips away.

St. Croix Middle School 3 — Cemetery Road Wanderers 4

14 Grandad

As we hurried back to the van, each of us still yelling and high-fiving and just hoping not to be told the game didn't count, a voice called through the open driver's window of a car, "Shay. Wait, please."

I stopped and looked around. Ms. Dugalici climbed from the car.

"Just a moment," she hissed at the others. "I know you're anxious to leave. I'll only keep Shay for a few seconds."

Ms. Dugalici folded her arms and leaned back against her car. "Miss Little's a good friend. I hope you appreciate her."

I nodded. "We all like Miss Little."

"She came to see me yesterday. She told me how you and your friends have broken all the rules in the Code of Conduct."

"They're stupid rules. Mr. Justason isn't being fair."

Ms. Dugalici held up a warning finger. "They're my rules, too."

I sighed.

Ms. Dugalici went on, "However, I have a suggestion. First, if you break the rules, you must accept the consequences."

"But —"

"Let me finish. Second, as captain — there are times when you must compromise."

"How do you mean?"

"By following the rules …"

"But …"

"… While I suggest to Mr. Justason that he modify them and reinstate your soccer team at the start of next season. You will also be allowed to play on the Back Field. How would that be?"

"That would be … brilliant. Thank you."

"Thank Miss Little for sticking up for you. Now — join your team, and tell them it's time to compromise."

I hesitated. Ms. Dugalici spoke in her usual threatening whisper and wore her usual mysterious dark glasses. She seemed the same severe person she had been when I'd seen her before. But she was being kind and helpful. I felt like apologizing for misjudging her.

"Why are you looking at me like that?" she demanded.

"I always thought you were scary."

"I am scary. You'd better believe it," she hissed sharply. Then she winked. "Now go."

Everyone was in the van, ready to leave.

"What did Ms. Dugalici want?" said Julie.

As she spoke, I noticed Mr. Justason and Mrs. Stuart steaming towards us.

"Hit it, Grease," I said urgently.

Mr. Finch called, "Congratulations on your win, although it won't count, and on being champions — for a little while, at least."

I heard Mr. Justason bawl, "I'll see all of you first thing in the morning—!"

The rest of his speech was drowned out by the screech of the van's tires as Grease wheeled out of the car park. Mr. Justason and Mrs. Stuart glared after us.

It was dusk by the time Grease rolled the van to a stop by the cemetery. Everybody scrambled out.

Jillian said, "Guess we better hurry home and face the music. Mom's sure going to be mad."

"Good luck," I called, as they set off.

Linh-Mai said, "Mom thinks I'm playing at the Back Field. I'd better hurry over there to meet her."

Brian said, "I'm meeting Dad on Main Street. Come on, Brandon. Dad will give you a ride home, too."

Grease held his hand out to Brandon and said, "Bye, buddy."

Brandon put his hand in Grease's and echoed, "B — ... Buddy."

As the Wanderers disappeared into the cemetery, Ice called after them, "Let's rock and roll again some time."

Soon, only Toby, Julie and I were left with Ice and Grease. We sat on the low wall that bordered the cemetery.

On the way back to Brunswick Valley in the van, Brian had interrogated Ice about where he'd learned to play soccer, and how he knew Jordan Thorne, until finally Ice had told us he'd played for the Montreal Marvels and had been signed by the Eastern Canadian Cougars, only to give it all up.

"But why?" Brian had persisted.

"Because I was always being compared to my father, and I knew I'd never be as good as him."

"Your father …" Brian's jaw had dropped. "You mean — is your father Dan Field? Wow! He's brilliant. Could you get his autograph for me?"

"See what I mean?" Ice had said bleakly before lapsing into silence.

Now I ventured carefully, "I don't care what you say about not being as good as your dad. You were a soccer star at the coaches competition, and I think you could be a soccer star with the Cougars."

"I could be a good league player — but never a star," said Ice.

"You're a star to us," said Julie softly.

"I saw the photos of you in your Montreal Marvels uniform at your house," I confessed.

"I suppose you saw the photos of my father, too."

"Yes. Then I saw him on television, and I guessed he was your dad soon after that."

"Your Grandad was a soccer star, too, wasn't he? My dad used to talk about him." Ice looked at me. "And you're real proud of him, and he's, like, an inspiration to you, and you're thinking my dad should be an inspiration to me, aren't you?"

"Something like that."

Ice shrugged and shook his head. "It doesn't always work that way."

"Was he disappointed when you gave up?"

"Was he ever. He hardly talked to me for a year. He still doesn't say much to me."

"Even if you don't want to play, you could coach," said Toby.

"You're a great coach," Julie added.

"That's what Miss Little said."

"When were you talking to Miss Little?" I asked.

"She was at the game. She recognized me from when I was in her kindergarten class at Brunswick Valley. She asked me if I'd help coach the soccer team when it started up again. She said she was sure you'd be playing next season."

"That'd be great," I said. "You might even start playing again."

Ice shrugged. "Maybe."

Grease had left the wall to tinker under the hood

of the van. He slammed it shut and joined us beside the cemetery gate.

I said, "Thanks for driving us around, Grease. We owe you."

Ice shook hands with Toby. "So long, Big T."

He offered his hand to Julie, saying, "You take care, darling."

She flew at him and hugged him. "You, too."

He held his hand out to me. "Stay cool, Shay. Seek glory!"

"Thanks for being our coach," I said.

"Thank you."

"What for?"

"For bringing me back to soccer."

We shook hands.

Ice said, "Let's go, Grease."

"Where to?"

"Main Street Parallel, I guess."

The van pulled away silently. "Cemetery Road Wanderers" was still painted on its sides.

We walked through the cemetery towards Main Street.

Julie said, "I don't know whether to wait for Mom to find out what happened or just go in and tell her myself."

"Glory always has a price," I said.

Just then Toby's step-dad pulled up beside us in his truck.

"I've been looking for you — ever since Mr. Justa-son called the house. Your ma's been worried."

"We were playing soccer at the Back Field," said Toby.

"No you weren't. For one thing — I checked there. And for another — you're suspended from play-ing soccer."

"Oh — yes. I forgot," said Toby. "We were …"

"Get in. Your ma's waiting — and she's not happy," said Conrad. He added, to Julie and me, "Do you want a ride?"

"We'll walk, thanks, Con," I said.

"You'd best get home fast. Your folks are waiting, too."

When we reached Julie's house, her mom was standing at the door, her hands on her hips. As soon as she saw us she started, "You can get yourself in here mighty fast, young lady. You've got some explaining to do."

I walked on in the dusk to my house. Through the front window, I could see Grandad in his armchair. I let myself quietly into the house — hoping he might be asleep. I peered in the dimly lit living room; Grandad didn't stir.

As I was about to creep upstairs, I heard, "Do you have something to say to me?"

I stood in the living room door. "I broke some rules at school, Grandad."

"I know."

"I got suspended from soccer."

"Uh-huh."

"And I lied to you."

"I know that, too."

"Sorry."

I crossed the room and leaned over the back of Grandad's chair. The book of poems was open on his lap. Over his shoulder, I read, "Between the mud and the sun, there are battles we've won. Ere shade ends our story, let's fashion brief glory."

"What rules did you break?" he asked.

"One about disruptive behaviour, one about wearing clothes that weren't suitable for school, one about keeping a good academic average, and another about inappropriate touching. Oh — and one about drugs."

"You took *drugs?*"

"No. Well, yes. Not really — just a mouthful of beer. It tasted awful. And I took a puff on a cigarette. I was mad about the rules."

"Were they good rules?"

"The rule about wearing clothes was an infringement of personal expression, and the rule about keeping an academic average of sixty-five isn't fair to students like Toby. He tries his best …"

"Anything else?"

"We broke the rule about touching when Julie *hugged* me, because she knew I was worried about you.

The rule about drugs is fair — we only broke that rule because I wanted to break them all."

"Why?"

"Because I was mad."

"You're in serious trouble at school, you know."

"Yes."

"Mr. Justason says he holds you responsible for what happened because you're the captain and you led the team in breaking the rules and deceiving the league and misrepresenting the school. He wants to know who was pretending to be your coach."

"I won't tell him."

"Come round here where I can see you," said Grandad.

I stood in front of him.

"So — because you thought these rules were an infringement of personal expression, and were unfair to struggling students, and stopped you having a little fun, you took it upon yourself to deliberately break them, and you led your friends to do the same."

I hung my head. "Yes."

"And although you knew right from the start that your protest was going to land your friends, as well as yourself, in serious trouble, and that whatever success your alternate soccer team enjoyed was going to be taken away from you by the league, you still led a kind of doomed rebellion."

"Yes," I whispered.

He stood slowly and put his hands on my shoulders.

"That's good," he said. "I'm proud of you."

Other books you'll enjoy in the Sports Stories series

Basketball

❏ *Courage on the Line* by Cynthia Bates #33
After Amelie changes schools, she must confront difficult former teammates in an extramural match.

❏ *Free Throw* by Jacqueline Guest #34
Matthew Eagletail must adjust to a new school, a new team and a new father along with five pesky sisters.

❏ *Triple Threat* by Jacqueline Guest #38
Matthew's cyber-pal Free Throw comes to visit, and together they face a bully on the court.

❏ *Queen of the Court* by Michele Martin Bossley #40
What happens when the school's fashion queen winds up on the basketball court?

❏ *Shooting Star* by Cynthia Bates #46
Quyen is dealing with a troublesome teammate on her new basketball team, as well as trouble at home. Her parents seem haunted by something that happened in Vietnam.

❏ *Home Court Advantage* by Sandra Diersch #51
Debbie had given up hope of being adopted, until the Lowells came along. Things were looking up, until Debbie is accused of stealing from the team.

❏ *Rebound* by Adrienne Mercer #54
C.J.'s dream in life is to play on the national basketball team. But one day she wakes up in pain and can barely move her joints, much less be a star player.

❏ *Out of Bounds* by Gunnery Sylvia #70
Jay must switch schools after a house fire. He must either give up the basketball season or play alongside his rival at his new school.

❑ *Personal Best* by Gunnery Sylvia #81
Jay is struggling with his running skills at basketball camp but luckily for Jay, a new teammate and friend has figured out how to bring out the best in people.

Ice Hockey

❑ *Shoot to Score* by Sandra Richmond #31
Playing defense on the B list alongside the coach's mean-spirited son is a tough obstacle for Steven to overcome, but he perseveres and changes his luck.

❑ *Brothers on Ice* by John Danakas #44
Brothers Dylan and Deke both want to play goal for the same team.

❑ *Rink Rivals* by Jacqueline Guest #49
A move to Calgary finds the Evans twins pitted against each other on the ice, and struggling to help each other out of trouble.

❑ *Power Play* by Michele Martin Bossley #50
An early-season injury causes Zach Thomas to play timidly, and a school bully just makes matters worse. Will a famous hockey player be able to help Zach sort things out?

❑ *Danger Zone* by Michele Martin Bossley #56
When Jason accidentally checks a player from behind, the boy is seriously hurt. Jason is devastated when the boy's parents want him suspended from the league.

❑ *A Goal in Sight* by Jacqueline Guest #57
When Aiden has to perform one hundred hours of community service, he is assigned to help a blind hockey player whose team is Calgary's Seeing Ice Dogs.

❑ *Ice Attack* by Beatrice Vandervelde #58
Alex and Bill used to be an unbeatable combination on the Lakers hockey team. Now that they are enemies, Alex is thinking about quitting.

❑ *Red-Line Blues* by Camilla Reghelini Rivers #59
Lee's hockey coach is only interested in the hotshots on his team. Ordinary players like him spend their time warming the bench.

❑ *Goon Squad* by Michele Martin Bossley #63
Jason knows he shouldn't play dirty, but the coach of his hockey team is telling him otherwise. This book is the exciting follow-up to *Power Play* and *Danger Zone*.

❑ *Interference* by Lorna Schultz Nicholson #68
Josh has finally made it to an elite hockey team, but his undiagnosed type one diabetes is working against him — and getting more serious by the day.

❑ *Deflection!* by Bill Swan #71
Jake and his two best friends play road hockey together and are members of the same league team. But some personal rivalries and interference from Jake's three all-too-supportive grandfathers start to create tension among the players.

❑ *Misconduct* by Beverly Scudamore #72
Matthew has always been a popular student and hockey player. But after an altercation with a tough kid named Dillon at hockey camp, Matt finds himself number one on the bully's hit list.

❑ *Roughing by Lorna Schultz Nicholson* #74
Josh is off to an elite hockey camp for the summer, where his roommate, Peter, is skilled enough to give Kevin, the star junior player, some serious competition, creating trouble on and off the ice.

❑ *Home Ice* by Beatrice Vandervelde #76
Leigh Aberdeen is determined to win the hockey championship with a new, all girls team, the Chinooks.

❑ *Against the Boards* by Lorna Schultz Nicholson #77
Peter has made it onto an AAA Bantam team and is now playing hockey in Edmonton. But this shy boy from the Northwest Territories is having a hard time adjusting to his new life.

❑ *Delaying the Game* by Lorna Schultz Nicholson #80
When Shane comes along, Kaleigh finds herself unsure whether she can balance hockey, her friendships, and this new dating-life.

❑ *Two on One* by C.A. Forsyth #83
When Jeff's hockey team gets a new coach, his sister Melody starts to get more attention as the team's shining talent.

❑ *Icebreaker* by Steven Barwin #88
Gregg Stokes can tell you exactly when his life took a turn for the worse. It was the day his new stepsister, Amy, joined the starting line-up of his hockey team.

❑ *Too Many Men* by Lorna Schultz Nicholson #89
Sam has just moved with his family to Ottawa. He's quickly made first goalie on the Kanata Kings, but he feels insecure about his place on the team and at school.

Soccer

❑ *Lizzie's Soccer Showdown* by John Danakas #3
When Lizzie asks why the boys and girls can't play together, she finds herself the new captain of the soccer team.

❑ *Alecia's Challenge* by Sandra Diersch #32
Thirteen-year-old Alecia has to cope with a new school, a new stepfather, and friends who have suddenly discovered the opposite sex.

❑ *Shut-Out!* by Camilla Reghelini Rivers #39
David wants to play soccer more than anything, but will the new coach let him?

❑ *Offside!* by Sandra Diersch #43
Alecia has to confront a new girl who drives her teammates crazy.

❑ *Heads Up!* by Dawn Hunter and Karen Hunter #45
Do the Warriors really need a new, hot-shot player who skips practice?